Prosperous
Friends

To Maggie + Daniel.
With delight

Prosperous Friends

to meet at this

CHRISTINE SCHUTT

Skylight reading!

Christine

Grove Press
New York

Permission to use an excerpt from "Transparent Window on a
Complex View" by Will Schutt was provided
by Yale University Press

A portion of this book originally appeared in *Harper's* magazine,
November 2009 and *NOON*

Published simultaneously in Canada
Printed in the United States of America

FIRST EDITION

ISBN-13: 978-0-8021-2038-0

Grove Press
an imprint of Grove/Atlantic, Inc.
841 Broadway
New York, NY 10003

Distributed by Publishers Group West

www.groveatlantic.com

12 13 14 15   10 9 8 7 6 5 4 3 2 1

To Diane Williams

Prosperous
Friends

Prologue

Such exorbitant crying! Just when the old woman thought she had stopped crying, the girl would start again. The sound raised in the old woman gladness and amazement, and she lay awake to listen, but all she heard was crying; the rest she made up.

Infidelity? Boredom?

The old woman went downstairs to turn off the lights left on for the young couple now upstairs. She went close to the registry to see their names, but decided not to look.

What else did the old woman let herself know? Their car was like everyone's car. New York plates. They were a couple; they had signed in under the same name. The girl's name started with a large and upright *I*, but she was not wearing a ring and the boy stood apart as if he were single. They were traveling to East Blue Hill but for how long was a question they had answered differently. The girl said maybe six weeks; the boy said three.

The boy, the old woman thought, was very pretty. A girl would cry over losing him, but this much?

The girl's kind of crying was at a pitch that befitted a graver occasion. The girl's crying was wholehearted, a baby's kind, in no way self-conscious; but unlike a baby's crying, the girl's had nothing to do with discomfort or hunger. Hers was purely announced sorrow.

The old woman had heard and so had the old man.

The old man, the next morning, looking at the ceiling, asked, "What was that last night?"

The old woman shook her head and said, "Wasn't it terrible?"

"So she wasn't moaning?"

"Honestly," the old woman said, and she looked back at where he lay with his hands behind his head. This was crying, the sound of which made the old woman believe that she, the girl, was in the right. Whatever cause was being fought, the girl deserved to win for her sincerity. Her swept, stripped crying was like an empty room, the boxy shadows on the walls, the unfaded parts against which beds and desks had pressed. Whoever had lived there, slept there, adjusted in front of a mirror there, was dead.

The rooms left by the old woman's dead are all yet unused. The closets are full; in a laundry basket still are her father's best shoes in shoe trees, a box, tissue paper.

Spendthrift mourner.

Ten years come August. She should clear out Daddy's room to add a room to the Wax Hill B & B.

Ed and Aura's is a farmhouse laddered with additions and trellises of clematis and roses; the inside walls are thin; the floors, slant. The rooms the Kyles let are low-ceilinged in the way of farmhouses, but the best of these, with the morning light, Aura gave to this couple. Aura gave the couple the whitest room because of the girl but also because of the boy. Aura had looked at the two when they were reading the brochures Aura always gives to guests. Aura considered their faces—they were probably not so young, not a girl and a boy, though she was of an age that turned everyone under forty into girls and boys, and so, too, these guests. The girl's straight eyebrows, her wide-open expression, the girl's face and the boy's face—she would not tire of looking at them.

No matter. The couple left the next morning. They left before breakfast, which Aura thought was wasteful.

Age is some of the story. Aura has a spot on her hand that she is watching grow. Halved in a fold of skin for a time, it has looked like shadow, but now the spot is larger and outstandingly itself; nevertheless, Aura believes only she knows the brown declivity for what it is.

Ed is eighty-two and proud of it.

Postdoc
London, 2002

The stone faces she saw on either side of the prior's door looked surprised.

She always expected grotesque but not so Ned, no. Ned Bourne was walking into the world with his arms open, whereas she, she suspected, everything she knew about people came from looking at them through a window. Now there was Ned to take her to sacred places, to the Ship of the Fens, a cathedral in the marshes. They stood on the threshold of the prior's door and felt how much cooler it was; the stones, cool and wet.

"Feel," Ned said, and Isabel held out her hand and touched the wall, clammy as a toad's but then think of all that had happened in this church!

"Come here," Ned said. He was braced in a corner in shadow. "Here," he said when she was closer. "Come here."

"Someone will see," she said even as she leaned against him and he rustled up her skirt. "Oh my, Ned!"

Ned, skilled in astonishment as from the start. "Really," she said, almost giving in to feeling but not quite— almost, nearly, a familiar breach in the intimate scene. She could only act excited, which he surely knew, and on the drive back to London, slashing past what they had passed before, the slurry view was all she saw: nothing still or edged but it was gone. Car turned in and paid for, day trip done.

"Let's go home," he said, and she looked up and saw he was far ahead. Why so fast, but Isabel Bourne caught up at the crosswalk and took hold of his hand and ran through the throbbing warning. A cold front or a damp front, in any case, a new front was coming in: The change for the worse in the weather chilled them. At home they drank soup and he sang aloud to her, " 'The grave's a fine and private place.' "

Night's disarray and rain and his disappointed face.

"What is it I can do for you, Isabel? What is it you need?" Ned asked.

If only she knew, but she never . . .

"Never?"

"Don't act as if this is news, Ned, please."

He took her hand and led her to bed and the cold ordeal of readying for bed, which was readying for something else, and she was not ready. "Relax," he said, and he worked to help her relax, stroked, kissed, used his hands inventively until after a while he rubbed himself against her mouth, her wet mouth moving, and the electric feather that was her tongue. He could, he could. "That's good what you're doing. Don't stop." And she didn't and he was satisfied. "But what can I do for you?"

If only there were something she could think of.

Las Vegas, a summer ago, 2001, she was up for anything—no matter the small results: early-bird special, Tex-Mex, fried. Las Vegas looked like Candyland but the colorless sky was a desert, and it was hot, hot. She had never been to Nevada—never to Utah or Wyoming, a lot of states, really, so they had meandered, Isabel Stark then and the persuasively all-to-everyone Ned Bourne.

How was it she was here with him now in London, but she was, she was Isabel Bourne, changed and unchanged. Already she had seen so much with him: the orange canyons of Zion and Bryce, where they had looked up silenced by slabs of righteous nature. In the weathering weather of Wyoming a girl needed steams and cold cream every night. The mountains, yes, the Tetons, yes, spectacular, goes without saying, but flat stretches of fenced-off pale land made for bleak memories, not a tree or animal in sight, only carcasses twisted in barbed wire.

"Nothing?" Ned asked, swinging away from her in the bed, seated at its edge, waiting for an answer that was no more than a smile at the sight of his muscled legs. She reached out and petted him.

"Whatever you're getting for yourself, get me some."

On that road trip across the country, they had sussed out state specialties but what were the English specialties? Toad in the hole, Cornish pasty, shepherd's pie, Ned had every intention of trying it all, bangers and mash, Stilton and port. In Minnesota they had discovered the pies were custardy, merangued, but what had been served up in South Dakota? Had they driven through at night? She remembered seeing buffalo. Buffalo in dirty coats slugging in the high grass—graceful, calm, as if eating were a kind of meditation.

Ned came back to bed with crisps, a noisy snack and a salty, smiley pleasure, a pleasure to be in his company although she was often out of his company that he might work without distraction. He had a fellowship and a book he hoped to finish, and Isabel? Since the ashy collapse of the year before, she could not find a subject large enough—arguments in kitchens and her parents' divorce? The time he almost left her but she cried and cried? Ned and Isabel often talked of the

event and other dilemmas of purpose and direction—
I'm not young! Isabel said, not a little surprised.

. ★

All too often a finger heavy on a key woke her, so
that she put the laptop on the floor and sat before a
pond of *yyyyyyyys*. Discomfort might keep her awake
if not her subject. "I need a regular job when we get
back," she said to herself and then later to Ned, "I need
a regular job when we get back to the States. I need
something to do."

Ned said, "Think of our time here as graduate
school"—no matter they had both just finished.

But graduate school had been so jokey. She had
honed skills in the thrift shops on Broadway, buying
furred sweaters and looking like Twiggy. And her thesis?
Isabel's stories? The criticisms from her classmates had
been spiteful or silly; the meanest of them closed on
upbeat notes: *Hope to read more!* Really? Ned's critiques
were smart. He hit on the weak spots in ways that
didn't shame her. Whatever brought on the sick-making
headaches was not much to do with Ned but sloth,
envy, anger, uncertainty. Why couldn't she live on a pot
of tea all morning and a mirthful meanness writing?

"So go out," he said. "Be courageous. See the city."

She went to the theater first. Isabel had dividends enough to see the same production of *The Seagull* as often as she liked, and she was enamored of its desperate Nina . . . "How sweet it used to be, Kostya! Remember? How bright, and warm, how joyous and pure our lives were!" Isabel had played Nina in a college production: ". . . a man comes along, by chance, and, because he has nothing better to do, destroys her . . ."

On the day Isabel came back from *The Seagull* a second time, Isabel wrote her father to thank him for his generosity. In a postscript she wrote, *Hello to Anabel.* "I've never written my stepmother's name before," Isabel said. "For that matter, I've never written to thank my father. This is progress, wouldn't you say?" She fanned herself with the letter.

"You're a kinder person, are you?" Ned said with an English inflection, so that it sounded like a question.

★

The next day, in studentlike spirit, to be smart, at times smart—Vassar was her own doing, had nothing to do with her father's money—Isabel went on a day trip to Cambridge with the Blue Guide and its rundown of the colleges and their famous members. Literary royalty—Milton had walked here. She unsettled herself with thoughts of sloughed-off skin on whatever had been touched. Maybe she would sit in some of Milton if she sat beneath the right tree in the right place. England's trees, and whoever met or dreamed, picnicked or loved beneath them, were a wonder: the enormous reach of copper beeches, explosive heads. Yews, chestnuts, limes, gingkos. The dead oaks in Windsor Great Park were no less than gods sycoraxed in a moment of anguish.

Might they not be released and made green again at some greater god's touch?

Anointment was what she sought, had sought. More than one visiting writer had said what matters most is staying in the room. She fell asleep in the room. Ned said, "Fine to stay in the room, but not all the time. You have to live." That's why she was drinking ale in the oldest pub in Cambridge, once known as The Eagle and Child, now just The Eagle with its RAF bar and plaques commemorating Watson and Crick, who drank here, talked, and thought. DNA—no small discovery. Isabel's great-grandfather on her father's side, Harley Chalmers Stark, came by a fortune through the garment trade and Wall Street; he was good with numbers, but Isabel was just so-so. The DNA got diluted, mixed up. From Isabel's mother's side came Eleanor, Isabel's grandmother. She wrote children's books. Her first and most popular book was published by a small press in Ohio. *Soap Bubbles for Christmas.* While Santa napped after his long night, the restless elves opened an unde-livered gift in the sleigh: soap bubbles. They romped in the snowy landscape, blowing bubbles that froze on the boughs of a pine tree. Jack Frost painted the bubbles bright colors. Remembering this book and its maker did not inspire confidence so much as admiration for the maker's use of her time. Isabel's father went to Harvard, but her mother studied French in a women's college that went out of business in 1982. Discomfited by the school's reputation, her mother's first disclaimer was *Don't ask me to speak French but I got an A.* Her mother did not inspire confidence. Why couldn't her mother have been an authority on something? A guy in the poetry division, August Mueller, had criticized Isabel for romanticizing the lives of artists. Artists were largely ignored, he scoffed; even if well funded, a group largely relevant only to themselves. Isabel had wanted to be an actress—was pretty enough but had not enough courage. Writing was hard. Ned had been the best of the writers in their year. Writing couples, how did they do it?

Isabel put the skinny triangles of bread on the side of her plate and ate the cheese and tomato.

One unexpectedly hot afternoon, she persuaded Ned to walk through Highgate Cemetery thinking it would make for the coolest exercise—reinvigorating, but it brought no extended relief. Ned complained. Better to be hot at home; at least there he could work. She was looking at the faithful mastiff at the foot of the pugilist's grave when the midget father appeared. Out of nowhere, an old-apple face on a little body, followed by a midget boy with hair like a cap pulled low. After that, Ned preferred walking in the wide spaces of heaths, views, Parliament Hill.

★

"I've got an idea," Ned said.

Lime House, when just a look could inspire anything.

Anything?

"How do you like this?"

"Yes, well. No, not exactly."

"How about this?"

"Yes."

"This?"

"A little."

"This?"

"No. No, that hurts. That really hurts, Ned!"

Afterward, the only thing he could say was he wanted to give her pleasure.

"Not that way, you don't."

She showered in a plugged-up tub, then sat growing colder in the scum that was water.

★

"Why is it so important to you?" Isabel asked.

"I think if you knew the sensation you'd want to have it more often."

★

A certain kind of woman—coarsely attractive, sensual, damp, bad skin—invariably told Isabel that Ned looked like an old boyfriend. Now, for instance, Sue Rassmussen was telling her how Ned looked just like this guy she knew back home in the States. Sue Rassmussen was talking about this guy, and as there was nothing expected of her in this conversation, Isabel turned away.

Of course, Isabel forgave Sue Rassmussen. Sue Rassmussen was only experiencing what others, what she, too, knew seeing Ned. He could quite literally stop conversation. Then again, Sue Rassmussen was a willful, aggressive, ugly woman. "'Ned looks like this guy I know.'" Who would believe it? Who cared?

"You don't have to come to these parties, Isabel": Ned at her ear.

Once at just such a party—people interested in Ned, friends with Ned, friends with friends of Ned— Isabel overheard Ned saying how lucky he was to look across at her every morning.

Did she really want to miss out on Ned making deep impressions?

Sue Rassmussen was at the party for Jonathan Loring, from Ned's class, whose memoir, *No One to Say It,* had just come out in Italian, and Jonathan, never modest, handed Isabel a copy to appreciate the gravity of its cover—not just the image—but the weight of the cover's paper itself. *Nessuno Lo Dice.* Jonathan said, "For Italians a book is a work of art."

"It's a nice-looking book," someone said, "but Italians don't read."

Sue Rassmussen was at the party where a woman leaned over the balcony, sick. The host, some new friend of Jonathan's—Carl?—ran down the stairs with a bucket of water he tossed at the bushes. He ran up and down the stairs with a bucket two or three times, puckishly apologizing, saying he was anal.

The party where Sue Rassmussen's conceit grew into a rash that Isabel scratched bloody was like so many of the parties Ned and Isabel went to, entered into together, moving around the room to talk to him and her and her. Once, a woman in an ash-colored alpaca sweater was the attraction for Isabel, but at the occasion where Isabel encountered Sue Rassmussen, there was no such woman in moon, ash, or evening colors.

★

"Let's just try this."

"I don't want to."

"Let's."

"No. Why don't you just give in to what I can do for you? Most guys would."

★

His idea had to do with women. Why did it surprise her? He had said as much before. Pick anyone in the theater was Ned's suggestion between acts, *The Maids*— very chilly. When she didn't pick, he did, and his choice alarmed her, but later she shut her eyes and imagined, even as Ned inventively opened her with his fingers and his tongue, imagined he was working on the young woman in the orchestra seat two rows ahead of them, a dark head of crimped hair that caught the light and looked wet. Isabel needed to touch it to know what it was about the wet hair on the small hard head between her legs; it was the girl's fingers Isabel held, not his.

"You were close, I thought."

"I thought, too."

★

But she thought a lot of things. She thought a girl who wore fishnet stockings and leather skirts would be discreet! Who was she kidding? G had an earring in her eyebrow. Her hair was the color of mud and dense; her breasts were no more than red cones. Her body was tough but her reactions to dogs, milk soap, cocoa were as goggly as her eyes. G was young; she missed camp. "S'mores," Isabel had said, "I know all about them."

"How did you meet this G?" he asked.

"How did we meet? We met here at the National Portrait Gallery. I was browsing in the gift shop. I was waiting for you then, too. She just started talking to me."

"About?"

"Her favorite portraits? I don't remember now, besides you're late, Ned."

"I'm sorry."

"It's all right."

He gave her the postcard G had sent of a naked old woman with a slab of paint for a pubis. The gray stroke could have been a headstone. On the back of the card in a hand hard to read was the message: " 'Flesh is the reason why oil painting was developed.' De Kooning. When are you going to let me do you?"

Isabel stood in front of Mary Wolstonecraft. The woman's forehead was serenely unlined although hadn't Godwin sullied her reputation?

"Fuck Godwin. Why didn't you tell me?"

"I'm telling you now. We met. It was nothing."

"Liar," he said, but his pretty mouth had a greasy shine as if he'd sucked on buttered toast.

But *it was nothing* was true. No more than a chance to sit in a bedsit, and there to kiss a young woman and watch her work at herself—*I like to be debased*. Was that it? Isabel had thought at the time. Far more instructive than G on that rainy afternoon had been seeing Ned in the evening. He didn't know her secret then, a secret ugly as a cyst was ugly or G was ugly, and that, Isabel had thought at the time, her secret, the elixir of betrayal, *was* exciting. But the days she accounted near perfect—and there were many of them—were book dry and predictable. They involved his reading in the morning and her writing awake at their shared desk, a walk after lunch,

PROSPEROUS FRIENDS   19

then her reading, his writing, and tea, and afterward more reading, sometimes to each other before the making of dinner. There were the cloudy afternoons, too, when she went to the British Museum and found perspective—*here I am; there they were*. She liked the centaur carved in high relief who was making away with a headless woman, but she ducked as through a tunnel past the brown disappointment of jewels like rusted nails, worn stone lions—abashed or indifferent or dumb—funerary kraters and Attic symbols, a cup, gold ingot, crushed. What was to be said about the gold cup but that someone very important lived in Kent thousands of years ago?

*

The girl Ned and Isabel had watched in the checkout line at Boots looked fourteen or fifteen, young. Her fingers were raw, the nails chewed and misshaped. Her hands were very small and, except for the fingertips, quite pale, and her arms were pale and led to the pale and hairless rest of her, there and there, or so Isabel thought.

Ned thought so, too. "Stand up," he said. "Turn around and let me shave you."

Isabel stood. She did as she was asked. These were the days when she was up to the humiliation of being handled all for nothing.

"Nothing?"

"What am I supposed to feel?"

"Oh, fuck it. As long as you're satisfied."

"And you're not?"

He was pinching her nipple.

This was an education, wasn't it.

★

"I'm sorry," she said.

"What for?"

"My mother."

"If I didn't believe in what I was doing," Ned said, and Isabel could hear that he was smiling next to her, behind her, very close in bed. Her mother's visit had been overlong, and their routine had been necessarily shelved to accommodate a chary woman, crammed with opinions but few questions. How could her mother resist Ned, but she did, had. Poor Mom.

Her mother, in a dust-colored dress, wore a face as inviting as a rake, yet why should the woman be enthusiastic about their marriage? Her mother's drama, the generic one: replaced by a younger version of herself rosy enough to wear red without in any way seeming menopausal. "Red is menopausal after forty," her mother said. She was probably right.

"My mother is scary."

"You're nothing like her."

"Really?"

Ned was holding Isabel in the narrow bed of her girlhood, or so she imagined, and she was a girl again and barefoot on the landing, her mother down the hall in an ataractic dark and all very quiet, the house, Isabel's. The chairs whined "pet me" and she ran her hand along the railings as she passed through the house, through the house and out the back door. She was moving quickly over the lawn, and when she looked back she saw her footprints in heavy trespass. Isabel lay on the stone bench in its ruff of thorns. The roses have a long reach!

"Careful."

"I'm being careful," he said.

Sharper inhalations in her girlhood's bed.

The sheets are heavy; the hour is wrong. "I'm all fucked up," she says.

"You'll get used to it."

She is already used to it.

"Stay with me now," Ned says. (Every part of her corked.) "Open your eyes. Look at me. Look at what we're doing."

He is quiet above her then, and maybe it's the way he is moving. . . .

"Concentrate!"

But she's a girl after all; she wanders; she makes things dewy. She gets overexcited! The noise, the bed—my mother!

★

It was that time of year, everything dying, when Isabel turned a corner and a blast of underground air at the newsstand made her sick.

"Isabel!"

She got as far as the chemist's when she rushed to the curb and bent over and spit. Something was happening to her.

The doctor's assessment was that she was two months gone.

That explained her breasts, their feverish bloat.

Ned and Isabel after the doctor, on the street, he had her arm.

She knew the night it happened. Whatever bird it was outside had sounded profound.

"I knew it," Isabel said to Ned.

"Hold on."

She was startled by the street but he knew where they were and promised to lead her toward refreshment.

"I don't want to make this into something it isn't," she said, but already she was remembering the granite bench in the garden, a bed and thorned and very exciting.

"Why not make it into something?"

"Well, then, it's a girl." Isabel was as sure of this as she was of the night it happened in the green conspiracy of midsummer's eve. There was an owl. The dark outside the window was not dark. There was a moon. The air was visible for all the noise in it, and they were in agreement, she and Ned, and nothing was needed beyond what they knew together, and all those fitful experiments, G and the rest, the urgency that drove them to know, to know, and for her sake, he said, especially, to experience. All they had thought necessary was not required! They'd made a girl that night. She knew.

The tea in the tea shop was mauve and hard to sweeten, but the shortbread popped in her mouth like a bag of powdered sugar, and Isabel was happy for a while to look across the table at her husband, for that was what he was, Ned Bourne, her husband.

"I can't do this now," she said.

He leaned forward to take her hand, but she pulled it away.

"Isabel," he said. He said it was all right. He said whatever she wanted to do, he understood.

She hated him for accommodating her.

The waitress came by but there was nothing they needed.

"No, wait. Do you have any honey?" Ned asked.

"I don't want to be sentimental," Isabel said.

"Be as sentimental as you like."

The honey spiraled into his tea.

"I can't do this," Isabel said.

Whatever she meant, he was behind her.

"Easy for you."

★

Isabel wanted to see the hyacinth macaws, the largest species of parrot, and one of the stars at the London Zoo, but size aside, the color of the bird was what she wanted to see. That they mated for life made them admirable, but were they really as blue as in the photographs? Yes, yes, yes. Self-possessed and regal. She had to turn away from the birds and walk ahead.

"Why are you so angry all of a sudden?" he asked.

"Why am I so angry? I don't know," she said. "I'm surprised, I'm surprised at how angry I am, but I am."

The bench they sat on was wet.

"Damn it." Isabel was thinking of her name, her maiden name, the name she hoped to call her professional name: Isabel Stark. Would their daughter be Stark-Bourne? Born stark naked was on her mind when she noticed the man walking toward them. He was unsteady on his feet, more a fluid than a man with bones. He was looking at Isabel and she was looking at him when he opened his coat and his zipper was down, and Isabel saw his malicious little cock.

Whatever happened, whatever she saw, whatever signage she read, the message applied, and to prove her point, Isabel stopped walking, turned, and read aloud the black hornbill's story: How the female is sealed in a tree on her nest for three months; only her bill pokes through so she can be fed. "I can't," she said. "I haven't become anything yet. I'd be a black hornbill sealed in a tree."

She said, "The hornbill sighting is telling me, don't do it."

"Don't what?" he said. "Come on."

Isabel was thirty-three years old. Her mother was twenty-two when she had had Isabel. Holly Mixon, her first-year roommate at Vassar, had two children already, and someone else from Isabel's class . . . who was it? She couldn't remember. Laura, her best friend, and room-mate for sophomore, junior, and senior years, was in Paris, childless. They had made promises to each other, promises to be purposeful, employed, well traveled. The

well-traveled part was under way, but purposeful or
employed?

"Are you so entirely happy," Isabel asked, and Ned
said, "I am. I'm up for anything!"

★

Of all the nightgowns to bring, this, the one ready to
be torn into rags. The nightgown bundled in her lap,
she saw, was her granny nightgown, yellowed under the
sleeves, and she couldn't quite understand her decision.

"Are you sure?" the doctor asked.

She did all the unsightly crying things, and both
men watched. She used the sleeve of her yellowed
nightgown on her face.

"You're in agreement?" the doctor asked.

"Yes," and they said yes at the same time, so Ned
and Isabel must have been in agreement.

★

So he didn't get what her problem was.

"You don't? Really? How many weeks has it
been?"

In truth, he couldn't remember what the doctor
looked like—only Isabel with a nightgown bundled

against her belly like a baby. Isabel, he remembered, and the Oriental carpet in the doctor's office, so old it looked black.

Ned said, "Look, Stahl's done a lot for me, and he's not here for very long, and I don't want you to come if you're going to shift into remote without warning."

"What?"

"You know what I mean, Isabel."

"You go," she said, for what had Stahl ever said to her but *You've a good name for a writer.*

★

Ned came home late but was not so tired as to refuse Isabel's request. "Make love to me, please," she said. He was obliging, so the night was shorter, though she slept and he didn't. His eyes smarted—pinpricked—as if he'd done all the crying. It hurt to close them, and he looked at the ceiling, at the wall, at the end of the bed, at the window beyond the end of the bed, and touring the room this way, he saw his jeans on the floor, stepped out of, small. He was weak—he had called Phoebe to congratulate her on her engagement—he was weak, and for all that his eyes hurt he mustered something watery that ran into his ears.

In the morning over coffee Isabel apologized for not being up to Stahl.

"He's important, you know."

"Impotent?"

Ned said, "If you could only look as if you were having fun, we might make some friends."

"I said I was sorry." Then, "Do you want more milk in that? Your coffee," she said, "it looks dark."

Turned away from him, she was an old woman, a bone, a crone, a downwardly sloped shape in a thin bathrobe, purposeless and derisible. Why this woman when there were so many others he might have amazed? So many he had amazed—even Phoebe, once Phoebe, especially Phoebe.

★

They went to a holiday party in Hammersmith in cowboy costumes.

"I couldn't resist a buckskin skirt," Isabel said, and she swirled to show off her fringe and knocked around in cowboy boots—a slutty shuffle, a hint that she was easy when they both knew she was not. No matter. She could not get the man's attention. The man's name was Fife and his face was all mouth.

"I know you from somewhere," he said to Ned. "I'm sure."

"Really?"

"Really," the man said, suggesting connections with names with connectives—the something von somethings, the something de Villes—on estates with escarpments, mottos, and wolf hounds. A royal charity, perhaps?

Who was this stuffed-up-sounding mouth breather, Fife, Fifidy-fife something, Simingdon Fife Fiefdom the second or the third. Whatever he was wearing for a costume approximated something formal.

"What are you?" Ned asked. "A conductor, a waiter?"

"An earl," he said, "an earl in real life. No, just kidding. I work at a bank."

Fife acted like a semiroyal. At the coat check he turned out his pockets and left a pile for a tip because the coins were too heavy and his suit was bespoke. The money was dirty, besides.

"I'll take you home," he said to Ned, and then to Isabel, "I sense your hesitation. I've a good driver. Don't worry."

"I'm not worried."

But Ned could see she was, and who was this man

really? He looked like Oscar Wilde, ungainly and full of appetite, but rich, there was that. Ned could see the money nudged against the curb and the driver on alert.

"After you," Fife said, and in Ned went and was instantly made imperishable in the vault of Fife's car.

"Is it German?"

"Why not?" Fife said.

And why not roughly, an all-night magic act willing girls? After a while, the girls got tired; nothing much was happening to them, and Isabel had no ideas. She seemed incapable of enjoying herself anywhere. She said, "I can't talk," but Ned waved her off.

She said, "Ned, please, Ned. Ned, Ned, Ned, Ned, Ned."

"You're such a drag," he said.

"Ned, Ned, Ned." Her voice was tiny and squeaky. She said, "I can't see!"

"Open your eyes!"

"I can't."

He led her out of the party and propped her against the building's gate. Told her to wait, he'd get a taxi.

The next thing he knew, there was Fife loudly returned to the street and undressing—at least he heard undressing sounds. Fife was shouting at Isabel to open her eyes and Isabel was making panicky squeaks, chittering like a squirrel. Fife had hold of her.

"Open your eyes, you dumb cunt!"

And she did and she puked on his shoes.

★

They came up with the idea of Rome together, Fife and Ned, and they all three took off for a week in December, but it rained most of the time and the discolored statuary looked like so much salvage in the dingy gush of water. So much for the city of fountains. At night the Piazza Navona twitched in gaseous light—they might have been in Las Vegas but for the sodden stalls of nativity scenes, carnival hawked: cheap. Even the church was dank despite the pulsing coils of heaters.

"Here, stand here," Ned said, and Isabel stood as near as she dared but was not warmed and said so.

"I'm cold, Ned, really."

Ned, however, Ned was irrepressibly hopped up, red, manic, an all-out tourist: Borromini, Rainaldi, Bernini.

Ah! Another bloody Christ, another bloody saint, another sepulchre of little bones brittle as brushwood: the tedium of martyrdoms. "I'm cold," Isabel said, "I'm going home," by which she meant the hotel on the hill overlooking the Spanish Steps, the Hassler, a brocade corruption enjoyed at someone else's expense, in this case, Fife's.

★

"Answer me, Ned. What are we doing with this man?"

"Getting out of the house," he said. "Isabel?" When she didn't answer, he reminded her of what he, Ned, had been good for: experience. And he wanted to see more and he was fascinated by this jaded, shallow man's bullying way of making money. And he didn't want to think about what might have been anymore. They had to believe they had made the right decision. "Isabel?"

She sat on the ledge of the sink and stuck out her face at the mirror, used a tweezers lightly.

Ned peed.

"Please," she said, distasteful twang in her voice. "I'll be finished in a minute."

"Fife's waiting."

"Let him wait."

Ned washed one hand and held the other indifferently over the patch between her legs.

"Make yourself at home," she said, worrying an eyebrow.

On his way out, he turned off the light.

"Hey!" she called after him. "I'm here, remember?"

★

Another night, another scrim walked through to darker places. Fife was dancing with Isabel—that much Ned knew—but where did the music come from? They didn't come back for dances. "Ages," he said, and Fife tapped Ned's forehead as if in blessing.

"You're ahead of us, Ned. What do you want, Isabel?"

"Water," she said. Then, "Don't whine, Ned. I only want water."

Fife moved down the bar, touching all he passed. Ned watched him, wonder-struck: Why had Isabel decided to dance with Fife? "Why did you?" he asked.

"He asked me," she said. Isabel's face was near his when she asked, "Some things that have happened between us should stay between us, don't you think?" She said, "It's okay to tell him I'm depressed—tell anyone, I don't care—but the reason? You don't know the reason, not really. There are a lot of reasons but only some of them have to do with you."

"With me, I hope," Fife said, taking a sip of his golden drink at the same time he handed Isabel a like drink.

"I asked for water," she said.

"Did you?"

Fife hitched Ned off the barstool and walked
him—talked him—to the back of the bar and into a
warm, wine-red leather space; Ned was in a womb or
a wound and Isabel was patting him. The next thing
he knew he was in bed at the hotel, alone in bed at the
hotel—same shirt and shorts but the rest of his costume
on the back of a chair.

"Isabel?"

No response but when he woke again, light bor-
dered the shuttered balcony and the bedroom was fully
returned, palpably quiet. He could see nothing had been
moved; his pants' legs still buckled off the back of the
chair, and outside he saw yet more rain. Was Rome always
this wet in December? Ned stood at the window, thank-
ful the room was generously heated and the accusatory
mirror that was his wife was turned away, a lot of hair
on a pillow. When had Isabel come back? It might be
his turn to play wronged, but had she been away at all?
Perhaps they had gone to bed together, or had she put
him to bed? He saw on the bedside table, his side, a
carafe of water and aspirin: She had thought of him. He
had done nothing for her but it was for himself, a self-
loathing mission, playing to an older man's desires—to
simply sit on the edge of their bed and talk and talk,
drinking bourbon—playing with Fife so as to see all he
could see at Fife's expense. On narrow streets mopeds,

like insects, screeched past and scared Isabel, and he knew, Ned knew she was scared, yet he did not wait for her. Now she was asleep and on his bedside table a carafe of water, aspirin. She had thought of him. That was nice. She was nice. Fife wanted to extend their vacation, go to Florence, see Ghiberti's doors. But Ned was thinking not today and maybe not on this trip.

"We've got the morning to ourselves," Ned said when he next woke. "Look, I'm all yours."

Afterward, they lay together and agreed that Fife was only fishy when he was drunk; then he was a fishy-fleshy sputterer. And his name wasn't Fife but Lewellan, which he hated, and so his friends called him Fife from Fifield, a middle name. Some friends called him Fife the third, and one of his oldest called him Life.

Ned sometimes called him Lew. He dialed his room and said, "Listen, Lew, Isabel's got one of her headaches, so we're staying in today. Depending on how she feels, maybe we'll have dinner."

Isabel silently cheered.

★

Ned had a lot of friends and they celebrated Boxing Day in Oxford on a walk with some of them from the night before. Isabel couldn't look at anything too closely for too long or else she was queasy from all she had had to drink while Ned's friends from Brown, Phoebe, and some guy named Straight, moved robustly—boastful of all they had consumed. A few others who had spent the night stayed behind. Phoebe was engaged to a lawyer, Ben Harris, whom she had left in New York to visit Oxford friends. She knew her way around and led Ned and Isabel and Straight blithely over the shivered lawn to Magdalen College and its deer park. The college was ancient but the frost was new, everything new and clean except that Isabel felt used and stale as if she had slept in her clothes. Then there was Ned with his flask. "Please, Ned. Must you?"

"Oh, a little taste of the night before never hurt, Izzie."

Ned pulled Isabel to him and turned her to face the deer. "Here's to a happy . . . ," he said just as a predator streaked over the fence and began to chase the small herd. They moved as a pack, one way, then another, but an outside doe was slower and slid, and the enormous dog, ugly as a jackal, cut her off.

Phoebe was calling out for a groundsman—was shouting to get a groundsman—*somebody!* And Ned was running toward the college, and Isabel? She watched, awash in the notion that this murder was somehow her fault. Ineffectual. All of them, ineffectual, even the groundsman, who ran toward them holding something like a weapon. By then the dog was at the doe's throat. There was the doe's rolling eye. The doe, still adorable, for all her terror.

This is hell—Isabel said. He could see how she fared and silently agreed: The savage dog had been an omen of worse to come. Ned knew she was thinking this then and later from the way she gripped her knife over brunch. What was it about this girl he had married?

"The cheese," Phoebe said. "Try the gray cheese. Trust me, it's delicious." Isabel appeared wary but smeared some of the gray cheese on the rim of her plate. The minced pie looked gaunt, and she moved past it to the bowl of fruit and cut a stem of grapes, gone-by globes, the fattest of them split.

"That's all you're going to have for dessert?" Phoebe asked. "Aren't you at least going to try Oliver's flan?" she said. Phoebe turned away from the buffet and came up behind Oliver, who was seated at the head of the table, and she kissed the top of his head and then turned back to the buffet and said, "The gray cheese, Ned, you've got to try it."

And Phoebe was right, the gray cheese—it looked like mold—was sweet, creamy. "Like brie but better," Ned said.

Why, Ned wondered, had Isabel bothered to come to Oxford? An assassin's face was sweeter than hers.

The yolk on the plates flaked off in the cleanup of the Boxing Day brunch, lunch—who cared when the food was so good? Not that Isabel had eaten much of it. Isabel was fading at the very moment everyone, and everyone at once, it seemed, had risen to help Oliver in the kitchen. Phoebe's job was napkins.

"Just napkins?" Isabel asked.

"I break things," Phoebe said and then to Straight, "and you're not so careful either."

When Ned next saw Isabel, she was kicking at the pebbled driveway and talking to Straight, a man she later described as in love with Phoebe.

"An old boyfriend," Ned said.

"You're an old boyfriend."

"What is it you want to say, Isabel?"

"I want to go home."

★

And then they were going home, the real one! Ned had his book, working title still a working title, *Lime House Stories,* and she had a guest book, a record of their guests at the real Lime House, the rental near Hampstead Heath. Its owners were in Israel. "Someday

I want to go to Israel," she said to Ned, then went back to the guest book.

I love you guys. Thanks for shelter. Jack Maas: Ned's cousin, his father's side.

"Aunt Charlotte," Ned said.

"Yes," she said. "The candlesticks."

"Do you really remember what people have sent us?"

"Of course," she said. "And if I'm not sure, I look it up."

"You've got a list?"

There in the Lime House guest book she saw her mother's adamant cursive: Mother/Beth. "Look at her signature, will you? Do you wonder I've got a list?"

She looked back at the signature. "From last October," Isabel said, "disastrous month."

"Let's not revisit it," Ned said.

Isabel read her roommate's message about their college pact to live abroad. "Oh, Laura! She has this gift of seeming interested in a person's life—she is interested! Laura is curious about people outside of herself. I don't have this gift," Isabel said. "I'm deeply incurious. Why are you smiling?"

Sam Solomon had signed her guest book. The weekend he spent with them he forgot he was running the tub—he was reading?—and he flooded their bathroom. And here was that friend of Ned's from Brown with the have-it-all smile and the large trust fund. "How could I forget Porter," she said, "but I did. Good artist, though," and she showed Ned the sketch of a house they both loved on Church Street in Hampstead.

"That would make a good cover," he said.

Isabel took back the guest book. Recipes exchanged. Phoebe's Pâté. *Cook in pan w/water. Don't pour off oil. Can freeze. Easy, of course! Enjoy!!* "Ick!" Isabel said. "I hated that liverwurst she made. You must have asked for this," Isabel said. Then, "What is she doing with Straight when she's marrying Ben Harris anyway?"

"Put the guest book away," Ned said. "If you need room for anything," he said, "I've got room in my bag."

★

London had happened so fast. Good-bye to the heath and the horse guards, to the floridly decorated flat. They were in the bedroom in Golders Green, alone, alone and together in the intimate familiar that was marriage—wasn't it? And she had nice clothes, too, didn't she?

"Come here," she said.

"Here?"

"Where else?"

"Isabel."

"What?"

"Do we have time for this?"

The White Street Loft
New York, 2003

"Right on time," a beige woman said, and, "I'm glad because it turns out I don't have a lot of time."

"Neither do I," Ned said, which wasn't true; the rest of his day, his week—his life!—was a blank, so he bucked up to make the most of it now with Carol, the woman in beige, who already knew the menu, though he asked for chili and a salad instead.

"Big mistake," she said. "Call the waiter back. "

"Too late—I'll live."

The commonplace salad came in the middle of an anecdote about antidepressants—"Had she lived," Ned was saying, "I don't know what my mother would have done with her time. I emptied the house when she died. I remember finding tooth whitener in her medicine cabinet; it was packaged like narcotics. The vials didn't have an expiration date. They were poisonous, I'm sure."

The woman in beige slapped away his hand. "Do you want some of my *frites*?" she asked.

"I do want some of your *freet,*" Ned said, and she swept some onto his plate, saying, "All you have to do is ask."

"That's enough," he said.

Carol got down to business then, talking and eating at the same time while he, uninterested in his insipid salad, ate her salty fries and watched the bracelet she wore slip up and down her arm as she cut into her skinny steak.

"Is that made out of coconut?" Ned pointed to the bracelet.

"Elk horn, thank you. Look—" She halted, ascertained. "Do you want to feel?" she asked as she slid the bracelet off her wrist.

He rubbed it with his thumb. "Neat."

"Look," she began again, "the stories are good, but a first collection of stories is a hard sell, think memoir." The beige woman used her knife efficiently. "That story you just told about your mother wasn't bad."

"What the hell," he said. The bangle didn't fit, and he gave it back to her, to Carol Bane—big-deal deal maker, Carol Bane. She was Stahl's agent, but the fat man was not off the mark when he described Carol Bane as deeply uninterested in books except to sell them, and this was true; she was a book-hating, hateful . . .

"Hey!" she slapped his hand again.

"The least you can do is share your fries," he said.

★

The phlegmy latch of complaint Ned coughed up all too frequently rose in his throat at the sight of his doctor.

Shouldn't he be finished talking about the family romance?

Of course not! Like a stern housekeeper, knock, knock, knocking an iron against a shirt, banged against and scorching the shirt, never once looking up at Ned, Dr. K said, "Of course not!"

Ned stared at a filing cabinet, as attractive as an air conditioner—a box with handles—hardly soothing. He coughed. He did the hitching trick with his throat to clear it more vehemently. "I never really looked at your furniture before. Like the bookcase in the waiting room," Ned said. "Where did that come from?"

"Where do you think it came from?"

"A lake house, that's where the bookcase came from. A wet place that never dried out, a snotty-slime slime-colored cube entered unwillingly though the lake itself was velvet. I know I'm talking about cunt," Ned said, and he reviled the attic-eclectic interior of Dr. K's waiting room. The glass-fronted bookcase, in its black, cracked veneer, a wood leached of light as if the bookcase had been drowned, recovered, used in the lake house for cook books and jelly jars—one full of pennies—the glass-fronted bookcase housed a set of cloth books, watermarked and faded. To the doctor's credit there were no Hieronymus Bosch prints, no ghastly garden of earthly delights.

"You make me more hateful than I am," Ned said, by way of good-bye, then shut the door. Hardly polite, hardly charming.

Hardly the way you were at the craft talk is what a student had said last night—hip bones like hooks when she shimmied past him at the bar. The student had left with a craftier talker. Ned didn't see, hadn't looked out for, after—hadn't what? Time was he would have taken advantage of a student.

Poor snake.

Ned walked down York, turned west onto a scabby street that should have been beautiful, not this mottled, unbuckled pavement, a narrow way all the way to a greater contraction, an underground entrance dank as the boathouse; subway stink and the usual terrors near the tracks before the train, and then he was on it—in it, a box that shunted downtown and made him faintly sick.

He once knew a girl with a crooked face—who was she? What did her eyebrows do?

"Isabel?"

The experience of calling after someone was an experience he no longer wanted to have. He was thirty-six. The fellowship that had funded him through Fife and London and Rome and Lime House was long since spent, so, too, his talents for attaching to comfortable people. With Stahl's help he turned onto the track of associate-something. . . .

"Give me a break," Isabel said. "Your thoughts are so depressingly obvious."

"You'll have to tell me because I don't know what it is I'm thinking."

"Working so hard, are you?"

Sometimes he came back to the White Street loft feeling good, but not today, which was a pity, for now there was the weekend to be got through in a rural part of New Jersey people did not mock. They were going to the country to see prosperous friends.

"Some fun," Isabel said.

"What is it with you?" Ned took up their bags—hers, unusually light. "Did you remember to pack warm clothes?"

"I remembered the first-aid kit."

The house they finally came to belonged to Ben Harris, Ben and Phoebe Harris now. The house, inherited, had three chimneys and outbuildings—a tool shed, a garage, a barn—all, like the house, painted white. The trees in the orchard were hoary with lichen, but the meadow, just mown, looked young. A picnic was shortly under way there, champagne and thawed hors d'oeuvres. Cheers to their prosperous friends! Ned chinged each glass, Phoebe's last. "How does it feel to be adored?" he asked.

"I'm used to it," Phoebe said. Then the torchy laugh—impossible not to smile although Isabel didn't; Isabel, eating a carrot, made bone-breaking sounds with her teeth.

"I like a girl who eats loudly," Ben said.

"Who do you remind me of?" Isabel asked. "Ned, who does Ben remind you of?"

He was wearily suspicious of the answer Isabel wanted and he would not—no, he shrugged. Ned wasn't going to revisit the site, remorselessly circle that spot where their life was stained . . . something to do with guilt and Hester Prynne feeling compelled to "haunt . . . the spot where some marked event had given color to her lifetime," and more lines from Hawthorne's novel he once knew by heart and which applied to Isabel now lugging that carcass onto the picnic blanket: *Lime House* and Fife and weeks of rain and the sulfurous sky of London at night—pink, unreal. He could not remember a single night of stars when they lived in Lime House, but they had made love in that house, he had tried—God knows. He'd have to look up that Hawthorne line once he got home.

"You don't have a copy of *The Scarlet Letter* here, do you?" he asked.

Not unless someone left a copy. Most of the books in the house were by writers out of fashion; a lot of books came from Ben's great-grandfather's library—but Hawthorne? "Wait," Ben said, and, good host, he loped, long-legged back to the house to look.

Again Phoebe's laugh, and it charmed Ned. "You," he said.

"We're getting old, Neddie."

"We're not."

"Then where's the urgent conversation?"

"Look what I found!" Ben was waving a book, no larger than a passport. *Tanglewood Tales,* Riverside Series, Houghton Mifflin. "Let's see. A gift to John Wren, 1913."

"Library smell," Ned said, with his nose inside the book. He gave it to Phoebe, and she smelled, too.

"The stacks," she said, "Mem Library."

Isabel said it smelled like kindergarten to her, like construction paper and paste.

So the talk bumped down stairs—from books, to the book, to *The Marble Faun,* to Italy. "We didn't tell you about Rome, did we?" So Phoebe began with a fennel dish. Their last best moment in Rome came down to food. "You remember, Ben? That place we found in the book?" The fennel dish she ordered was to start; it came hot in a little ramekin with Parmesan, raisins, and something else. Pine nuts? "I meant to remember. It was so good. The only reason we didn't gain weight was because we walked miles every day, starting early in the morning." The streets were washed and cool then, and the jasmine—that was everywhere— didn't overwhelm them with its scent.

"When we were in Rome, it rained most of the time, but we did a lot of walking," Isabel said. "We walked over six miles one day from the Spanish Steps to the Protestant Cemetery to see the poets' headstones— and that was just in an afternoon."

"You went with Fife," Ned said.

"So?"

Phoebe and Ben had been in Rome for a wedding. A wedding in ivories and greens—deep, and deeper. The ceremony was in the afternoon on a formal lawn, cypress trees, hedges, a goldfish pond. Greek classic— the bride looked like Aphrodite in a generously pleated, high-waisted gown; in her hair, a wreath of ivory flowers, the same in the bouquet. The light was salmony. Orange made small appearances everywhere all night—orange being the bride and groom's favorite color.

"A favorite color," Ben said.

"We don't have one," Phoebe said, "if you're wondering."

"Look!" Isabel said, real surprise in her voice, surprise and something else—delight? She was on her knees. "Look what I found in the grass," and she held out her palm.

"What is it?" Ned asked.

Ben looked closely into her cupped hands. "A baby mouse," he said, "at least that's what I think it is."

"Awful! Get rid of it," Phoebe said.

"I can't do that."

Ned looked again and saw that the pink knob was, yes, probably a mouse, a hairless runt, jostled from the rodents' wagon-train retreat. Why leave the nest at all, he wondered, but that the afterbirth that slicked the nest might have drawn predators—who knows? "You could put it there," Ned suggested to Isabel.

"What?"

"Under the tree over there, next to the roots, cover it up with leaves. Its mother might come back."

"Are you crazy?"

He watched as Isabel took the infant mouse into the house. Phoebe stood to follow. "I'll go," Ned said, and he started after Isabel, calling her name. "Isabel?"

Inside, Ned watched as she turned her side of the room, the guest room, into a close, incubated space.

"What are you doing?" Ned watched as she moved the decorative bedside lamp and put in its place the desk lamp with the arm bent low so the halogen might gently warm him—him?

"It's a rodent, for God's sake."

"I need an eyedropper," she said, "and some warmed-up milk. No sugar," she said.

"You're crazy," he said. "Use your first-aid kit. I'm going back outside."

But Phoebe and Ben were carrying the picnic, or what was left of the picnic, inside. Ben was going into town to get charcoal; Ned intended to stay near the mouse emergency, but in the end he stayed near Phoebe. On the screened porch, drinking rum, he sat with Phoebe while his wife ministered to a mouse. Upstairs in the guest room Isabel was squeezing milk onto the pink knob's face or its anus—drowning what was already dead? He confessed it saddened him that he and Isabel were past caring about appearances.

"Stop fretting," Phoebe said. "Come with me. You haven't had the tour."

Phoebe walked him through the oldest parts of the manse she had married; a bricked-up fireplace accounted for one of the chimneys in what could have been a breakfast room off the summer kitchen—*Imagine, two kitchens!*—so many rooms and so many of them unused. No, Phoebe had never thought of marriage in terms of sets of china; she was a bit overwhelmed. "But I love it," she said. "More of everything—look!" He pressed against the old glass and saw the barn from the work-room window. "Yes," she said, "the barn." But first the summer kitchen and its narrowing to the fix-it room made greasy as a pipe for all its use.

"Not here," she whispered. Her lipsticked lips against his ear. "Here," she said, and the newly married Mrs. Benjamin Chester-Harris threw up her arm as she might toss away a hat, and she was his old flame again, Phoebe, a sly shepherdess—hardly dumb—in Ned's arms in yet another room of indeterminate use but for chairs and windows and there, as abruptly situated as a closet, a bathroom only big enough for elves.

"My God!"The sink—for a child?—came to Ned's knees.

"Quick," Phoebe said.

★

Sometime in the middle of a dreamless night, Ned woke to Isabel crying into a towel she held over her face. He thought he had been gentle enough, wishing her good night, and quiet enough when he finally came to bed, so that to see her awake now—"What's the problem?"—awake and at the jagged end of crying, trying to catch her breath, to speak, to say, "Nothing, nothing's the matter." She yawned and yawned until, visibly composed, no longer out of breath, she said, "I'm not crying over you if that's what you think. You can do as you please."

If the rodent wasn't dead then, it was dead by morning. It was gone from the room, the bedside table cleared, and the lamps returned to their rightful places; Isabel, fully dressed, sat composed in a chair, reading a book on terror. Breakfast with the host and hostess was equally sedate. *The New York Times* was on the table, a bowl of grapes, cheeses, salami, hard-boiled eggs, and bread.

"I'm still in Italy," Phoebe said.

In the car, Isabel remarked on Phoebe's ass. Salami and cheese are not the breakfast foods she should be having. So the cheerless drive home began.

★

Why not compound defeat was Ned's response two weeks later, when he came home to a blind dog of uncertain age, a shih tzu mixed with something, so sick upon rescue, Isabel had thought to return him, but it was too late now with the dog in her lap and the loft's lights dimmed. She was smiling in the corner near her desk where she had made up a crate. She had sprayed her own perfume onto the fleecy mat, so the dog might know her.

"If it makes you happy," he said. Met with a dog less alive than a stuffed one and just as pliable, Ned could only say, "If this is what it takes, if it makes you this happy."

She said it did make her happy although she did not sound convinced. Isabel held the dog close—spoke softly to him about going to bed. The scene was dismal, and Ned sighed to see the dog let himself be fitted into the crate. Then for a while it seemed the dog was awake. Hard to tell. Ned had yet to get too near the crate.

"I almost forgot. Doggie bag!" he said and held up the dessert he had ordered over lunch. "I didn't eat it and Carol never finishes hers." Carrot cake, wrapped separately, and crème brûlée, skidding in its container: two of Isabel's favorite sweets.

"I thought you just had lunch with Carol," she said. "Why were you having lunch with Carol?"

"Why do I always have lunch with Carol?" was the answer he gave even as he saw Phoebe ask the waiter, please, could he make a doggie bag?

Now Ned put the desserts out on separate plates. "We could do this for dinner."

"I don't have anything else in mind," Isabel said.

So they drank red wine and shared the carrot cake—"So good," Isabel said—and she came around the table and kneaded Ned's shoulders.

Her being nice made Ned feel guilty about seeing Phoebe—God knows, not Carol—but when he remembered the blind shih tzu and the fact of Isabel's touching him after cold dinners, no dinners, silence and silence, it annoyed him.

"Thank you for letting me foster this dog," she said, and she kissed his cheek.

"Do I have a choice?"

"You sound tired."

"I am."

Her joyless "All righty."

"What is it now, Isabel? Huh?"

The grunting of the disgruntled; they're both too tired to fight.

Later, they lay in bed listening to the dog's wheezy breathing. "Will you help me?" she asked. "If we could just do this one thing together, I think. . . ."

He could hear in her voice that she was as lonely as he was, but for answer he could only say her name, "Isabel"—an equivocal answer at best.

★

Ned saw the dead eye, a pink glistening marble, and the other an otherworldly blue, cataracted, scratched. The dog was in pain and made the most tormented cries. The head doctor whose name came first on the board though he wore blue jeans and a checked shirt and eschewed a white coat, the head vet came in to see if the younger vet attending the dog, a pale girl with a tiny face and enormous eyebrows, had applied a topical anesthetic. Ned didn't understand her answer, but he liked the skinny boy in the green outfit, even though the green outfit suggested he was only a helper, an assistant—not a real vet. The head vet looked as if he should be fishing whereas the helper was doing the difficult work. He was holding the dog, and over its screams he was joshing, calling the dog "BK," an upbeat endearment, a twist on Brooklyn, the name the pound had given this desolate being because the blind shih tzu had been found in Brooklyn on Neptune Avenue, a stray.

Then the girl vet poked out pellets of impacted crap, which explained the dog's great thirst. Unplugged, BK wagged his tail for the first time since Ned had known him.

But a week later, the vet informed them that BK's blood indicated the start of kidney failure. More tests were necessary. And the very next morning, Isabel carried BK back to the vet where she was given new pills for the dog on top of the other, and Puralube ointment, an ocular lubricant for the cataracted eye. In the loft BK mostly slept.

"Peanut butter," Ned said, and he proffered the dog a dollop of Jif stuck with pills and in this way learned how easy it was to give BK his medicine.

"What next?" he asked.

"I think the dog is deaf."

"Why?"

"Maybe dim then."

"Maybe."

"No, deaf." And she lifted him, a soft sack of something living—(Ned saw the dog's face only once; full side, eye open, the opalescent, not the red.) Isabel set the dog to stand on the floor and turned him to face the wall, which he did in a sweet dumb trance that wasn't broken by the sound of the vacuum or tin bowls banged together. BK didn't hear; the dog didn't turn around.

The dog died, he crossed the Rainbow Bridge, but before that, Ned took him every day for a week to the vet's in a precautionary manner; hopeful—well, and desirous of the veterinarians' company, especially the boy in the green operating duds although the boy really wasn't a boy, only his sweet exuberance marked him as a boy.

"It looks to me as if you'd owned that dog for years," the boy had said that first visit.

Ned liked the boy but the vet's office was dirty and preposterously small. The two examining rooms were the size of a closet. In one, another young assistant—in green, blue, white duds?—was eating lunch off the step-on scale. She had made a plate out of the hamburger's wrapping—but to eat in the same room where dogs sneezed and cat parings black as a mechanic's flicked into space and landed on the step-on scale, where even now the assistant was craning to catch the mayonnaise leaking from one side of a hamburger so big it had to be a Whopper. The vet they had found was unsanitary. At the checkout station, desultory biscuits decomposed in a jar—shit. What was he doing here with the dog in his arms, handing the dog over, when he really wanted to be talked out of it or into it, but the fucking vet, the one who belonged in Montana braining trout with rocks, was in a rush and he jabbed the sedative needle in and the dog yelped and then yielded up himself.

Why didn't Ned turn away from, take the dog away from, but he walked out and for a moment, yes, a moment, he was free!

Now, days later, what he couldn't quell was the horror of his turning away from a messenger, surely a god in disguise—the old lady who had stopped him on the street just as he had turned away from the dog groomer's and decided on the vet, the old lady approached and in a voice full of tears asked, "May I pet your dog, please?" She said to the blind dog, "Oh, I had one like you." She said, "Oh, so wonderful. Aren't they wonderful? Isn't he wonderful?"

"He's blind," Ned said.

"Oh," she said with a shrug, "that happens."

"He's also deaf."

The old lady said, "But he can feel, can't he?"

★

"Who?" he asked.

Phoebe held up a finger and spoke into the phone in her soberest voice about looking at the Schumacher. Ned didn't know what would be looked at, but he wasn't interested enough to ask was it a faucet or a couch?

"It never ceases to amaze me that people live like this," he said when he had Phoebe's full attention.

She wondered that he had never been to the apartment before. "Are you sure?" She swiveled in her chair and inventoried her in-home office. "Doesn't any of this look familiar?"

He started to say, "Aside from the mess, but no. No," he said, and then he saw the familiar photograph of the cottage on the bluff overlooking the Menemsha Harbor. "Martha's Vineyard," he said. Sea glass in the soap dish and Phoebe's dormered bedroom, close, churchy, hot. "I remember."

"I should hope so," Phoebe said. "I'm going in July—we are." She said, "Now, what can I do for you, sir?"

"For starters?"

"For starters," Phoebe said, "I'm very much my own woman today."

"No clients?"

"Not today. Not unless I decide to see the Schumacher—patterns," she said, "material."

"See me," he said. "I put the dog down today."

They had the afternoon to themselves and could, given overcast weather, guiltlessly cavort through most of it. How better to spend the time? For years, he had been impersonating a disciplined writer, putting off pleasure until the cocktail hour—so why not now run his hand along her check, touch her collar bone, her breast . . . ?

"Why'd you stop?" Phoebe asked.

"I go about my business so glumly."

"This isn't getting you down," she said and her merry expression when she tugged at him made him smile.

When had Isabel stopped smiling?

★

Back at the White Street loft he saw Isabel sitting on the floor next to the shih tzu's empty crate.

The empty crate brought back the anguish of that morning, the empty crate and the fleecy bedding, the tin bowl of water, the water slopped onto the floor as if someone had just been drinking from the bowl, as if the dog were still with them and not, as Ned remembered, remembered all too easily and readily, not a helpless animal on his side, wide-eyed—that blue marble Ned had seen for the one and only time—not an animal relieved. Relieved? Who would wish to be relieved of his aches, small and large, if it meant death? Relieved of being purely a heart without the distraction of sight and hearing, just a beating heart. Ned's own was beating in his ears.

"I'm sorry," Isabel said.

"I need to be happy more of the time," he said, making as if to rub his nose, smelling Phoebe on his fingers.

"We both."

But having been happy for most of the afternoon, it was easier for him now to go over to the crate and collapse it. He put the fleece into a plastic bag to be washed separately, and he took up the water bowl and the food bowl and washed them at the sink. He gave Isabel the tube of lavender incense sticks and told her to light one or two—"Clear the air," he said—but he was muddled by discovery of a stuffed toy, just a shape really, like a scepter with ears, Isabel's purchase in her willfully blind expectation that the blind dog would play fetch. Where to put the fucking toy? Didn't they know a deserving dog or two?—theirs, a childless, dog-less marriage. Maybe someone had cats?

"Why not a cat next time?" he said.

"I don't want a next time," Isabel said. "I'm poison."

The White Street Loft
New York, 2004

If a street had seasons, White Street was early spring, too colorless, hardly sentimental, no budded touches, nothing risen but March, secular and cruel. To think she had lived on this street for almost two years when the plan had been to rent the loft for six months, meanwhile look around to buy, get permanent. Oh, what was she doing? Shaking her bag for the sound of her keys to get into the loft quickly. The space was dark, though known, and she ran through it to where the oven hood shone holy. Weirdly overheated, she ran cold water over her wrists. "Too much excitement," she said aloud to herself, and felt the water's sting and wondered if, when Ned came home tonight, she would tell him about Clive Harris calling.

But why do that? G, remember G? But this was different. G was no more than a punk girl in a bedsit; whereas Clive Harris, well, Clive Harris was older, established, a painter with a following. He came from money and had kept it. Think of James Merrill, James Merrill, a patrician poet of the last century—"a relic," a classmate had said although Isabel found him attractive. Those artists with their attendant wives, partners, mistresses, muses, observing summer's gyre in inherited homes on islands and coasts—that was the sweet life, wasn't it? James Merrill in a documentary wore a white bathrobe, or was it a kimono? The taut cords in his thin neck pulsed when he spoke in his aristocratic voice. To admit to being transported by the sound of his voice—was she elitist and out of date? Maybe, probably. But why tell Ned of Clive except to stir in him some feeling for her as at the beginning, when anything was possible. Then if he so much as caught her staring at him—the book she was reading no more than a fan—he often put down his own book and went to where she was sitting and put his head in her lap.

Relief not to be hungry at all but rather pleasantly distracted by the body's other parts. Nipples, for example, hers prickled, and she touched herself and leaned into the corner of her desk, and she played—the way she remembered as a kid, skipping little words over the placid future: *ram, cat, slut, cunt*—rubbed against the corner of her desk. If Clive were only a woman was a thought that was pleasurable.

Clive Harris, at his nephew's marriage to Phoebe
Chester—over a year ago, February? She had not forgotten. Clive Harris had pulled her up against the old
club's coffered wall to save her from the press of the
tuxedo crowd. "To see the club's library, a woman must
be escorted by a member," he said. "Would you like
to see it?"

"Would I?"

Real excitement at a wedding at last!

★

After breakfast—skipped—Isabel stood at the long
closet mirror. She looked just as she had hoped to
look when being nasty to Ned, lovely, at ease. Waste
of time to be mean, but when had she ever been
wise? She had kissed another man, not her husband,
at a wedding, which was not a big deal, except that
today she hoped to kiss this man again with clearer
intentions. She had really almost forgotten him. Clive
Harris, he said in a voice unused to being forgotten. The Union Club. Ben and Phoebe's wedding,
remember? She remembered. Also the visit to Ben and
Phoebe's, the mouse, and a moment when she stood
at the guest-room window looking out at Ben Harris,
some distance from the house in the vegetable garden,

practicing good husbandry with a rake and seeds. His long reach and the steady way he worked. Ben Harris was a good man, and his uncle, Clive Harris, the painter, was he so very good? Her own reflection in any surface was most often pleasurable—except that she was too fat! Too fat! But Fife had said, "You're skinny enough, just dull."

Now there was tonight with Clive Harris at a restaurant in Midtown, but she had plans she had to change first. She explained to Ned that she had been invited to dinner by Ben Harris's uncle, Clive Harris, and that, in the flush of the invitation, she had forgotten about the reading. "I'm sorry to miss him," Isabel said, then, "but this way you and Stahl can really talk. And who knows?" *Who knows* was an inducement to go anywhere, meet anyone, try anything, but his easy acquiescence to her absence made her wonder: What event was it first diluted the marriage, or was it an absence of event, Isabel's failure to make something worth regarding? Where was her book, her business, her flaring discovery? She spoke no other languages, had no hobbies—unless reading was a hobby. She was paid like a hobbiest in the freelancing world. Also she tutored. She had work.

★

"You put me in mind of my daughter," Clive said. "You're about the same age."

"I'm thirty-four," Isabel Bourne said.

"Right," he said. "Sally's forty. I'm glad you look surprised." Clive leaned across the table nearer to Isabel. He knuckled her cheek: How warm she was, blushing. Their waiter was smitten, too, and directed his attention solely to Isabel and talked at length of what could be had from the dessert case. According to the waiter, there was, yes, indeed, an eight-layer cake if she cared to look.

But no, she didn't.

"I trust you," Clive said, and the waiter seemed surprised to see Clive and noted the order as if calculating all—eight layers, fifteen dollars, plus wine, sea bass, a decorative appetizer, how old—how much was that? Clive might have been Isabel's father.

"Clive?" she asked.

"Isabel? I bet they have sorbet."

"Orange, raspberry, lemon, coconut."

"Raspberry," she said to their careful waiter, who bowed and backed away.

A halfhearted restaurant with swagged Arthurian touches—torchlights and crests, blood-brown carpeting—only the tapestries of courtly love and valor were missing. He thought of dungeons, plagues, Boccaccio and his pigs: Stink was linked to putrefaction;

putrefaction to pestilence; a pleasant smell meant puri-
fied. Isabel's hand was all lily of the valley and clean;
her nails were shell. "You are inspiring," he said, "but
this restaurant we've found . . ."

"Is silly," she said.

Clive smelled her hand once again, and the restaurant turned buoyant, and the service, the service
was, well, here came their waiter with dessert already:
the eight-layer cake, white with red filling, wedding-
like and flouncy on a tablecloth scraped so clean that
the dinner seemed to be starting again, and Isabel was
saying she would like it to start again. "And I'm not
fond of Wednesdays."

"Ah, hah."

"Would there be anything else?"

"No thank you."

"I'm baffled," she said once the waiter had left.
"You baffle me."

Not a remark to answer, but Clive smiled at the
small hook Isabel used to catch him. He, a ravaged
carp, practiced in taking advantage of the stunned or
wounded, although his appetite, of late, had dulled.
And why cloak his intentions so darkly? He wanted
to be kind if only Isabel would hold still and let him
look at her: bark-brown hair and eyes; eyes wide apart,
pale face.

"What about your wife?" she asked.

"What about my wife?"

They stood on the sidewalk, empty taxis passing. "What's her name?" Isabel asked.

"Dinah," he said.

"I've never known a Dinah before," she said.

"Now you do," he said. "It's a name people like to say."

He made a large, showy whistle and a cab swerved in with accompanying verve, and Clive offered her up and sent her home. The cabdriver was on the phone speaking in a furious language, and Isabel was glad to get out of the cab, away from the close, coarse—too mortal—smells, his and her own. The cloudy partition, his impossible name. Only the turban helped. A Sikh.

Poughkeepsie first, then London, now the city Nick Carraway liked, and she still saw the world as through a window. Why couldn't she be like F. Scott Fitzgerald, or maybe she was like Fitzgerald, and "both enchanted and repelled by the inexhaustible variety of life."

On her way to the tutoring center the next afternoon, hot spots in the making bristled high inside her legs and it took all the willpower she could muster to keep from wheedling her hand down her tights to press her cooler fingers against the heat of what was happening: hives, scrofulous signs she saw when she chugged down her tights in the ladies', hot, dime-size, repellent pustules—pink, itchy—high on the inside of her legs. Hives. "Fuck me!" And she scratched at the hives until they popped, like blisters, with warm blistery water inside. So much for sitting comfortably with the dull boy Adam. Did he like *The Great Gatsby*? The two-hour session heaved along and she really couldn't tell. Adam read so flatly she took over, so what did they learn together, she doing most of the talking, both of them wriggling in their seats?

Once home, she drank soup and took hot baths but still felt dirty. Worse, Clive Harris did not call, not the next day or the next, so was it any wonder she got sick? Here again were the near-dead, weird days when she lived as in a closet in her migraine hell: her bed, a box of rags; her heart, a corner, spooky. Sometime in the night—the next night, the next day?—Ned crossed the room; then the room emptied of people, and Isabel shut her eyes but they wouldn't stop working: The pink underside of her eyelids, a million pixels, blinked; the sight made her sick, but when she opened her eyes, she turned sicker—always the way with her.

★

"Clive?" The curtains in the bedroom were drawn, and she was speaking softly from her bed.

"Isabel?"

"My God, this phone is heavy."

"Isabel," he began, but she had to hang up, and when the phone began to ring again, she pulled out the cord. Had she called him or he her?

★

There was weather outside and she asked Ned to describe it.

"Milky sunshine," he said.

"What?"

"That's what I heard on the radio this morning."

"My skull," Isabel said, "it feels vacuumed."

She thought Ned would say yes if she asked him to stay but she didn't ask; she waited until she was sure he was gone. "Ned?" The answering silence was sweet then and she slept.

This time—but what time was that?—she answered the phone and heard Clive's voice.

Oh, come over, come over and look me over the way you did! If only she knew what to say. The phone was in her hand. Was that all? Would that be all? I'm feeling better? Now, when her body was ringing, why weren't they making plans for the future?

But she was feeling better.

★

And Ned wasn't surprised at her recovery. Isabel was not one to miss a play, especially if she liked the actors. And the actors! But after the play so often came the theater fug. On this night, Ned and Isabel walked and talked about the famous actress and how she had used her hands to convey Mary Tyrone's suffering. Isabel was moved by it, but her heart really went out to Jamie. "He is the sufferer; Edmund can write and has this thing with his mother." Ned gave Isabel his handkerchief, and she used it and said, "Oh, that was sad, that was stunning, that was terrible. Families. Oh, God!"

"You okay?"

"Hardly." The way the actress had used her hands —those palsied gestures—how pitiably empty they were, the hands and the gestures. To see a great performance is a gift from the gods and she remembered the heart-wrecked peacock king with the golden round in his hand—Richard, the poet, in tears, defeated, talking of the death of kings. This was at the Globe; Isabel had stalked him, the actor, stalked in her fashion, prowling the frowsy stalls of tourist traps for pictures of him and greats aged or dead, old programs and photographs, anything to do with the small-seeming actor who played the king or any of the other odd crushes then in England on the Lime House adventure. Harold Pinter, Harold Pinter. The lascivious peeper in *No Man's Land* says "what is obligatory to keep in your vision is space, space in moonlight particularly, and lots of it." No moles, no nose hairs, no moon-pit pores. Isabel had considered this idea on more than one occasion and was relieved to feel still young enough that it did not quite apply to her. The fishtail lines at her eyes were faint; they didn't last beyond her smile, and she didn't smile much, not in Ned's company, anyway, not much anymore—why?

Ned, not for the first time, sat on the edge of their bed and said, "You're going to have to be the initiator."

O, so bring out the three-prong speculum, the ratchet-mouth gag, the diddle kit, and forceps.

"You're easy to please," he said.

So she had always believed.

★

Clive Harris blew at his coffee and looked at the mess on his daughter's plate. First time together in New York since Ben's wedding last year, and already Sally was glum. He said, "There are people in the world who love you, Sally, and want you well and happy."

Sally said she was fine; really, she was fine and she smiled and sipped water and turned the crust of her potpie into crumbs as she described her day thus far. A grotesquely crippled French woman from Algeria had shared at the meeting the astonishing fact that she could not drink water straight. Water by itself made her sick. She couldn't stand the taste. The French accent made her story more convincing. Also the French woman had a beautiful face—there was Arab in it—but no legs to speak of, little stumps in corrective boots. However could she have had babies? Sally asked. "I mean, I wonder," and she looked at Clive.

"Terrible!" she said.

Sally was changing doctors and medication again.

"It takes about six weeks to get happy," Sally said, and she pulled her sweater tighter and shivered although the diner was warm and served jolly food—comfort food most called it: potpies, meatloafs, creamed spinach. Alas, no good desserts, and Sally? Sally cried.

Clive handed her a handkerchief.

"You know what it is?"

"What?" he asked.

"I need to sit under a sunlamp for a couple of hours every day."

Sally, Sally, Sally, shaped like an egg, warm brown and large, he wondered at her: AA meetings and cripples. Why should it be but that she was ungainly, shy, unsure, a girl, a woman really, a woman with some talent·

daughter—and quite alone but for sharing her problems with strangers? Something about Sally—there was the will to fail or did he mean flail? Headaches—he didn't want to know about headaches or pills and sunlamps and whatever the hell it took to get happy.

The girls Clive had known—so many girls, where were they? Where were the girls who had found their way into his room when he was a boy, sixteen, great age—everything worked.

Clive almost wished Sally drank. Now she was speedy and loud, a little overeager to share her miseries, turning to the biggest, her mother, Clive's first wife, Margaret, called Meg. Meg had been a drinker, which explained why, a few years earlier, on a simple midday errand, the poor woman had been stalled, arrested as by air, confused—which way headed? Westport, Connecticut, August 1999. First stroke. Just before the millennium and the destruction of the towers.

Sally exhaled—to heck with the diet—and she took up her fork and so came the story of the mean and practiced child moving fast as a rat along a wall doing damage. "Yesterday Wisia told me she wanted to staple my mouth shut. Do I sound desperate? 'Go live with your other mother,' I tell her. 'You can rip up things together.'"

Clive put out his hand, saying, "Sally."

"That scares the kid. That shuts her up!" Sally said, "I haven't seen you in so long."

"That's not true," Clive said.

"It's always true. So much happens and you're out of touch. We kept Mom for a while, you know. I thought I didn't want her in a nursing home, but in the house she was a banshee." Naked—enough to sear the eyes!—Mom had wandered naked into the kitchen and slipped and fell. "Wisia was in the kitchen with me at the time and she threw herself onto her grandmother as if the woman were a sandpile, which was how she looked, like a sandpile of flesh."

"Please," Clive said, "don't tell me these things."

"Does this mean you won't visit her?"

"Calm down," Clive said.

"Am I right, you won't?"

He said. "You're right."

"I'm right about it being a long time since we talked, too." And when he didn't answer, she asked, "You're staying on, aren't you? You're not going back right away?"

"Calm down, Sally," he said. "I leave Thursday. We could take a walk tomorrow in the park if you like."

"Meet at Bethesda Terrace?" she asked.

"Okay," he said. "Now isn't that worth a smile?" But Sally didn't smile right away, thinking of her mother, no doubt, of Meg. "I've been thinking," but Clive didn't tell her of what. "Poor Sally," he said. "What would you like to do for the next hour?"

"Skip town. Buy a ticket to some warm island. Otherwise, shopping."

"Anything in particular?"

"Not that I can think of."

"Buy Dinah a post card," he said.

"Find something for Wisia, too," he said.

Something soft, Sally thought, and childish. And Dinah? A card she had seen once would be perfect: King Kong with Fay Wray in his grip.

★

Clive, at the top of the stairs to the terrace, saw Sally walking toward the angel in a large coat that looked like something her mother might have worn. (He should give Sally the money he knew she needed.) Sally's mother, a long unbuttoned girl swinging bell-like and wide, had once walked willingly, smilingly toward him—for an entire roll of film, she moved agreeably among the pigeons. Ah, *acqua alta* in the Piazza San Marco, all awash yet staunchly swept, and the coffee-house, famous. He saw in his daughter his once-cheerful wife, Meg, in the piazza, winter, a happy winter for them both despite a year of crepe and tears. That first

Christmas after Clive's father's death when his mother had asked him please, couldn't we all do something other than New York, far away but family?

Italy then.

On a colder afternoon, Clive and Meg shut their shared umbrella and shook themselves out at the araby that was the entrance to the Caffè Florian. *Here we are! Sorry!* Hardly sorry, but bed-warm beneath their coats. "We were happy," Clive said to Sally now. "Your mother and I, and we made my mother happy, too, at a time when, I think, she didn't expect to feel much of anything." Across a room, distantly tinseled—bar pin, bracelet, ring—his mother once at the Hotel Gritti on the Grand Canal, New Year's Eve, a widow in a loose sheath, black—black beaded; she sat uncertainly holding a flute of something pingy. At his father's memorial service, his mother had told Clive not to expect such a turnout for her—and there wasn't.

In a companionable moment, he put his arm around the soft shape of his daughter. The bowed softness of his daughter, the cushioned arms, not his mother's arms or his, but hers, Sally's. Children are always entirely themselves—so Dinah said. Dinah, his second, sturdy wife, he missed her.

As if his daughter knew his thoughts, she asked after Dinah.

"Dinah is fine," he said, with some relief to be walking in the sun, walking north, northeast from Bethesda Terrace to the Conservatory Garden, some considerable distance, though he was fit, Clive; he still ran. He was ready for spring. Dinah was crazed for it but otherwise fine.

"There's already spring interest here. Look at that!" he said.

The early dogwood's yellow had arrived, no more than dots on twigs, yet they brightened the bark-chip mulch and blackened leaves that had toughed out winter. He liked the yellows better than the pinks to come or the Conservatory Garden's rigid plantings of tulips, now just spikes, but the penitent Lenten rose was up in borders, and he liked that perennial very much.

"Look inside," he said, and Sally bent down next to Clive and looked inside the surprise of the muted hellebore.

They had seen more spring than he had expected. "That was pleasant," he said and meant it, glad not to have talked about money or that woman Sally lived with—anything to do with Sally's messy grown-up life.

"I thought we could pick up Wisia at school together" was Sally's hopeful invitation at the gates to the Conservatory Garden.

But no, he couldn't come to school. A friend had called, not someone she knew.

"Man or woman?"

"What business is it of yours?"

"Why won't you see Mom?"

The answer he had was too harsh, and he didn't know why he went ahead and said, "For the same reason I don't see you that often. You both make me sad."

"If you think we're disappointing, Dad. Really, to be stingy at your age."

He made as if to take off her head and didn't stop short but hit her in the neck with his hand. He hit her but not that hard.

"That hurt."

"Wasn't very hard."

"Says who?" Sally backed into the street and waved down a cab, all the while holding a hand against her neck. "Enjoy the rest of your visit," Sally said, before she shut the door.

He would. Goddamn her. He had perversely persevered, had lunched, dined, breakfasted with Sally, walked with Sally, listened to her litany of insufficiencies—starting with funds! He could have been seeing Isabel Bourne. His surprise was considerable then when Sally appeared the next day at Torvold's gallery. She startled them both, Clive and the convincing young adult (spotty beard but deep voice) there to interview Clive. "This is a surprise." Clive stood up. "My daughter," Clive said, by way of introduction to the young man named . . . he'd already forgotten.

"I'm sorry," she said to the young man and then again to both of them. "Really, I am." Sally looked closely at her watch, pressed her ear to the face of it. "Go ahead," she said, then, "Oh, no, is that recording?"

"No," the young man said. "No, I turned it off."

"Lucky," she said although it seemed to Clive she was the unluckiest person. She was too timorous to make a wider way through the world, yet it gladdened him to know he was predominant still and could shut her up with just a look. Clive sternly watched her walk to the other end of the gallery with its glassy island of a table and low seating that conformed to it. Onto this shoreline Sally dropped as if she had been pushed.

"I'll just wait," she said, and she took off her watch and peered closely at it, longer than was necessary, and she did not look back at Clive; rather, she seemed to be talking to her watch. Had she been drinking? He wasn't going to give her any more money no matter what it was for.

The interviewer, ever hopeful, said, "Italy?"

Yes. His mother had taken him. He was eight years old and he liked looking at paintings, especially the noisy terrors recorded in Renaissance paintings, paintings of those suspect and traitorous early Christians so inventively tortured, drawn and quartered, boiled, burned, defenestrated. Some figures had no more dimension than drapery, flayed as they were or flung from the Tarpeian Rock. The dogs, unleashed, were outraged, bullet-headed hounds in the likeness of Cerberus—savage mouths.

"I couldn't stop looking," Clive said, although his own horrible imaginings dismayed him. Now, for instance, he thought of Sally and the ways she might be hurt, had been hurt—on her own, by him, by others. The bruise on her neck had a black center she should have concealed—it was not becoming. Why didn't she know? She was forty and he was . . . didn't matter; work was life's imperative. Wisia was eight— his age when first he saw Pauline Borghese. Such a slender invitation, breasts no more than suggestions, Canova's Pauline reclined on her marble chaise under a vague wrap.

Clive talked about the massacre of the innocents, another image first encountered with his mother in Italy. He had always suspected adults of violence, but up until then he had not seen that much of it. His own parents were model and kind. (In truth, his mother was neither, but Clive felt no obligation to be truthful.)

A gunshot. That's what it sounded like when Sally dropped the heavy coffee-table book on the floor.

"If there's a better time," the young man said.

"No, no, no, no, no. Now is fine," he said, but he could hear at the other end of the gallery, Sally was making those sounds he knew for the mewling preamble to *I'm sad. I'm tired. I'm sorry,* though she didn't mean it. Clive moved his chair closer to the young man, saying, "I'm not going to look back at her." But he was looking back. Yesterday in a flirtatious coat, she had swayed for attention. *Look at me, listen to me, help me:* the tedious refrain to Sally's song of herself. Her neediness unsettled him or was it unseated him?

But he talked on. He had given so many interviews in his lifetime: Clive had grown up in Boston, which was as far as he went besides acknowledging he had had parents. He liked to hint at having known harder times as if his impeccable academic background had come by way of scholarships. "I've a brother and a sister, both older, not artists." He had loved to draw from the beginning, but from whom had he inherited his gift? His mother, yes, she had had such ambitions.

"I should add my father was an architect of some distinction." Why did he say this now—a fact known but not uttered by him in past interviews—why except that Sally was present and he hoped she was listening, oh, how many times had he told his daughter yearning was all very fine but only the doing counted?

Sally banged the book shut.

Clive said, "My feeling about form is that it's discovered. My friend P. A. Ricks says the same is true of fiction—not an original idea." Yes, Clive knew a lot of writers; his wife, Dinah, was a poet.

If Dinah could see now how Sally lumbered around the glass island to look at the gallery's paintings, Dinah wouldn't wonder at his reluctance to see more of his daughter. Clive called out, "I don't think Torvold wants us in his offices, Sally."

Why did he have to speak to her as if she were twelve years old?

To have an awkward daughter came as a surprise. How often Sally stood too close to a person, bumped into railings, stumbled. He was afraid for her—and for the glass table and the cylindrical vase of calla lilies. She should not be near anything that wasn't planted in the ground.

What was on his mind, the young man asked, when he painted the white horse series?

"Not much," he said. "The palette changes." That was vague; he turned quotable. The horses were the visual equivalent of his state of mind at the time he painted them. The source of his pain was too petty to relate. "When I was in California, I did a lot of sketches of horses. Horses are very beautiful to me, even the most ragged has a soulful expression."

Sally loved the horses; she *had* one of the paintings.

"One winter when my wife and I were house-bound, I painted the horses. All the different shades of white outside and inside were a comfort and a drag."

"So the landscape informed your 'white' period?"

"Death," Clive said, "informs everything I see."

Were artists relevant, could they instruct?

That was not the point. When he was painting, Clive said, he wasn't thinking about meaning; he was looking to feel something.

Clive had said all there was to say, and if the young man had to end on a light note, well, he could finish the interview with a description of the scene, old man in the foreground and, behind, the suggestion of a woman on a Barcelona couch; both just strokes of paint, faces vacant.

"You've been more than generous with your time," the young man said, and he stood and looked to the other end of the bleached wood and white gallery and waved good-bye to Sally, who came forward after the young man had left.

"I called Dinah," she said. "She said you're going to invite a complete stranger to live in the Bridge House for the summer."

"Isabel Bourne is not a stranger."

"I bet," Sally said.

★

Ned was in Boston, or so he had told Isabel when Clive came to the White Street loft. He came with chicken soup and wonky cheeses packed in grass, the Easter-basket kind.

"Wasted on you," he said. "I know your type."

"What was it reminded you of me?" she asked him.

He had been thinking of her. He wanted to paint her. She would have time alone, too, to write. She could stay in the Bridge House.

"But your daughter . . ."

"The Bridge House is mine," he said. He described an old house, barely furnished; the kitchen counter tin and patched in places. The house was empty for a couple of years while the original owner was in the nursing home. She was the last of her line. "For a while it looked as if the house might be left to fall but a goddaughter

was willed it. She sold it from afar, cheaply. There is no
bridge. Dinah made up the name: the Bridge House
for a house without a bridge. Our own house doesn't
have a name. We've a stone wall, a barn for me to paint
in, and Dinah's garden. Why are you smiling?"

"What about your wife? What about Ned? Why
do you think I would do this?" she asked.

"I don't know," Clive said. "Most people I invite
say yes."

Noisy moths battered the barn light in her brain as
he talked about firefly season. Not to be missed, and the
light, especially in the afternoon, in the late afternoon,
he described the way it turned their bedroom pink.

"Why are you telling me this?"

The phone rang and rang and rang until the
answering machine clicked, and they heard Ned saying, "This should make you happy . . ." before Isabel
muted the machine. "I'll find out later," she said, "and
it won't make me happy, I'm sure."

"But be happy now," Clive said. "Come sit next
to me. I'll be quiet."

In Clive Harris she had found a new album in
which to put any pictures she wanted: a white pitcher
of cream on a round table, covered in a checkered
cloth, two skinny French park chairs unevenly settled
on the pebbled path. Where was this? France, Spain,

Italy? France. Nice—Neese. To say *nice* seemed cornball, but that was Clive to her.

"I am not nice," he said. He was thinking of Sally, poor Sally and the drab adjectives he used whenever he spoke of what she was but might have been.

An only, lonely daughter. "I am one of those, and Ned is an only, too. Maybe that's why," but she didn't finish.

Clive's brother was unwell but his sister was in remarkable health. "We speak on the holidays," he said. "Dinah sends her something she's dried or canned or sewn along with an explanation about whether you wear it or eat it or hook it on a nail. Last year she cured *Nepeta*—catnip—and sent it to Gwen, who has a Maine coon the size of a bear. Bangor's his name and he's old and sleeps all the time, at least he did. Gwen sprinkled Dinah's cat elixir on his paws, and instantly Bangor was a new man, gurgling and bumping around the house, positively happy, humming."

She was humming, too, with her arm held out and Clive petting it as he talked his way closer. He held her breasts, assessed what parts of her there were to be assessed, unbuttoning, pulling her shirt off her shoulder. "Let me admire," he said, and he looked for what seemed a long time, and she looked down, too, at a small lacy triangle of a brassiere, a cocoa-colored whiff of lingerie. Clive's hand against her collarbone, she took it up and put it against her face and smelled him in a brandy fume of sensations before his hands against her head guided her downward to disappointment: Why did it always end like this with that musty part in her mouth?

"Ah," he said, finished, "you wish it could be more."

"I don't know."

"I know," Clive said, using his shirt as a towel.

He left not long after. He left saying nothing more of Maine but that he wanted Isabel to know he was, as ever, an admirer. He would like to paint her.

"Maybe," she said aloud after he had gone.

Water runneled down the windows or else lights jiggled in the wind—something streaked the view. Her eyes burned and she hated the sky, starless, cloaked, low, wet, cold, oh, what did she have to be sad about really. *I wanted to be an actress but I was too shy.* What a stupid, phony admission. In London she could have taken classes. *I once sat next to Rufus Sewell at the Royal Court.* There was a moment! "I tutor," she had said. "I'm not a teacher." At least she was honest about that. "I think about writing fiction, but then I look at how miserable it's making Ned." Clive must have kissed her on the forehead then.

★

Ned, back in New York, no more than a day, said, "We've been invited to this party."

"Who invited us?" Isabel asked.

"Does it matter? It's ice-skating, Izzie. A little break from sloth and contemplation."

Ned was right; the new someone knew someone who knew someone; it was one of those parties, but she hadn't expected to see Phoebe there, Phoebe and Ben, Ben skating at such an angle it looked as if his cheek would touch the ice. *I went to tennis camp with his brother* she overheard. Were there other conversations she might intrude on?

A nameless Dartmouth man spurted ice shavings in his showy stop at her feet. He was a hotshot ice-skater, face as common as a pit bull's but large and friendly, a panting invitation: "Do you want to impress your husband and try some tricks with me?"

Did she ever!

The Dartmouth man said, "Just hold on."

Here were the words she had lived by uttered by a Dartmouth man moving her around the rink at a speed never before reached in all her years of skating—if that was what she had been doing, skating. Had she ever been spun quite like this or lifted?

"Look at what your wife can do!" the Dartmouth man hollered as he skated off and around the ring fast.

"Nothing I didn't know already," Ned said, and his tone was encouraging when she had hoped for sour. It seemed he was not worried about her daring turns but skated freely, unpartnered until Phoebe, out of nowhere, found him. Now he stood on the other side of the ice, listening to Phoebe talk. His mouth wasn't moving and Phoebe was making small circles, head held down, yet Isabel was trying to read Phoebe's movements to know what she was saying when the Dartmouth man showed up again for more tricks!

★

Ned and Isabel, days after skating, midweek, after another night at the theater: "'If this be so, why blame you me to love you?'" Said again, said faster, fast but differently, sensibly stressed:

"'If this be so, why blame you me to love you?'"
"'If this be so, why blame you me to love you?'"
Ned was first to phumpher.
"F–U–M–F–U–R?"

"Spell it any way you like. It's a made-up word," Isabel said. "I can only find *fumble* in it, so I'm not sure it qualifies as a portmanteau. Maybe like *buzz,* maybe onomatopoeia? Our drama teacher used it whenever we botched a speech."

Ned carried on with the speech in more of a whisper, said, "And so am I for Phoebe . . ." And on the instant in his expression was real dolor and not just because of the unseasonable cold or the letdown at the end of great theater, but because of the utterance. *Phoebe.*

" 'Maids are May when they are maids but the sky changes when they are wives.' I like melancholy," Isabel said.

"That's one of the problems," Ned said. "I want to be happy more of the time."

"You don't say," Isabel said.

The spell of Rosalind in the round dispelled, Isabel and Ned rocked on their heels in the subway station, waiting for the train to Manhattan and the White Street loft, home.

★

Oh, to feel buoyant as a cork in choppy water! Phoebe, of course he thought of Phoebe when he said her name. Her name was the first thing about her Ned loved. She had been obscured by a man as big as a rowboat—no one could have seen past him—Phoebe was obscured despite the high-heeled boots she was wearing then. (Phoebe always in standout clothes.) Phoebe liked high heels. "I like tottering," she told him long after he had heard her name. "Phoebe!" The first he knew of her at Porter Blaire's twenty-first birthday party, hundreds of Porter's friends, Phoebe among them and the rowboat. Ned pressed in to see when he heard her smoker's voice. So her voice was the second thing he loved; third was the girl herself, entire: Phoebe in high-heeled boots that came over her knees and fit tightly and tight jeans and an Aran Isle sweater so old the sleeves were stiff. Except for the boots, she could have come in from cutting turf or mucking stalls. Maybe she had; she smelled cold, and her hair, always harsh, was it tangled up with straw? It looked scratchy—was scratchy, he was certain, and they hadn't even met.

"This is our stop," Isabel said.

"Already?" He was surprised and surprised again when she told him about the Bridge House and Clive. The Bridge House on offer was free. A free house with a view of the ocean! Usually it was Ned who gilded their lives. Now the Bridge House, not far from but out of sight of Clive's, was situated on the coastline by itself with only one other house in view and that one, sadly, an eyesore, Weed's Mechanics, car parts and sheds on the waterside, too, but to the north of them, so the ocean was unobstructed. The mutable Atlantic matched the sky.

"I'm his muse at the moment. Does that surprise you?"

"It doesn't surprise me."

"You should see your face," Isabel said, but he was intrigued and looking for his reflection in the half-moon window, finding it, seeming to approve before he looked at her.

She did not want to spend the summer in New York. "Remember last summer?" For Isabel last summer's discomfort peaked on a humid weekend in Tuxedo Park, mixed doubles. She played with Porter; Ned, with Porter's date. Porter carried Isabel through to the finals, but she had muffed a drop shot. Runner-up was not what Porter had in mind.

"Do you think Porter Blaire will ever get married?"

"Where did that come from?" Ned asked.

No answer but she shrugged, free-falling into disparate, general thoughts. The Bridge House was free, a little tottery, perhaps, and peaked—no, no? The Bridge House, gray as a garden bench—"It's really yellow," Clive had said—but to her it was gray and in places mixed with pink. Behind the clouds was light while here on earth the ocean riffled over the granite stoop.

Married, what was it to be happily married? The poor couple in the Greek myth, granted any wish, asked that they might die together and so they did. The gods turned the old couple into a miracle—one trunk, two trees, a linden and an oak.

"Clive is happily married," she said, and a part of her believed it true and that she, Isabel, was no more than a passing thought. But might not Ned see her worth in Clive's eyes? "You should come with me," she said.

★

"I was early," Ned said, considering Carol Bane, his agent, forever in beige. What color skin was best for beige? Not hers. A bloodless, bleached woman whose body had surely never known a vivid day—a goblet grace maybe, once, for her wedding—today she wore sand-colored clothes as shapeless as dunes and large bangles; the impression she made was disingenuously indecisive. The waiter had told them the specials, then left them with menus. She pushed his newest story in its sleeve across the table.

"Once again," Carol Bane said, "a second book of stories is not a good idea. Make it a memoir."

They looked at their menus, shut their menus.

"Do you know what you want?" Ned asked her.

The waiter recited the day's specials a second time, to which Carol Bane responded, "Nothing much to shout about is there?"

Carol Bane hesitated, and he wondered if she was not well. After a certain age—what the fuck did that mean, a certain age? He couldn't keep up her pace in the prickly heat, though he tried. He walked from Broadway and 45th to 125th. There in a studio he worked on the manuscript Carol Bane had returned. A Whiting is all very fine but fiction is a hard sell and hard fiction, short fiction, well . . . He could fix this; he could be less elliptical; he could be faithful to Isabel and disciplined. The Bridge House, as he understood it, was a loosely amorous residence open to artists, and he was an artist, wasn't he? And Isabel was his wife, wasn't she? He thought about his classmate Jonathan Loring and his big-deal memoir, *No One to Say It*—hah! Loring's quick and unequivocal *you're fucked* to Ned's marriage. *Some guys like projects*. But there was more to Isabel than project. Her expressive face with its many lovely registers—an actress's face, had she the courage—was a face responsive to him. *Lime House* was as much her book . . . no. She had been there with him when he wrote it. Now he would write a memoir. Once, he had thought about being a poet, but he couldn't scan, a fact that seemed fatal at twenty. Dinah Harris was a poet; he had seen her name in *New Yorker* font. Was it a poem taped to a season, was that it, something to do with jack-o'-lanterns and death? He could write any-where, or so he told Isabel when he came home from lunch with Carol Bane. He told Isabel he would write a memoir at the Bridge House. "You said I could come."

The Bridge House
Maine, 2004

The unmanning memory of the Clam Box. The Clam Box on the dock, that lidded, sunken, mossy place, hurried, humid, steaming tubs of shellfish, small orange light; it was here they all sat—two, three nights ago.

"Don't," Isabel had advised Ned behind their menus.

"Don't what?"

"Oh, to hell with it. Do what you want."

He had shown off. Good schoolboy, having done his homework and up to date on Clive's opinions, full of praise for de Kooning: "firsthand, deep and clear." He, Ned, wanted to be intense like de Kooning's colors and intense, intensely himself. Homer, Marin? The muddy sea? And why not? No doubt, he was a bore. "I really can't remember a fucking thing," he said.

Oh, God! Turning from these considerations, he makes his way across a room of shirtfronts and bare arms. He is looking for Isabel, who has disappeared. Light fizzes. Someone taps his shoulder and he turns and sees the only crone in the room with skin as luminous as coal, dry patches, and above her upper lip, small hairs.

This old woman with the mustache keeps turning up.

"I'm spooked," he says, relieved to see the woman at the window is Isabel, shoulder blades sawing, skeletally illustrative of the puppet body. There are many reasons Isabel does not eat; she has told him a few. At the Clam Box, for instance, there had been no green on the table that Isabel could see. First the gray steamers, then the lobsters, looking maniacal next to the alarming corn.

Ned had been all right until he saw him. Ned had muddled the face of the handsome old man, Clive Harris, high color and white hair, hair curled over his collar, puffed out, sort of wild. The hair and the faded clothes Harris wore and the way he stood made him out to be unusually hardy at seventy-some years old. How had Ned forgotten this man, Ben Harris's uncle, but Ned had been looking at Phoebe. Didn't everyone look at the bride? Now, it seemed, everyone looked at Clive Harris, the best known of well-known painters on the peninsula—sure, showy, famous. Famous? No. Isabel was wrong about that. The tourists didn't really turn around to see Clive Harris. Clive Harris and his wife, just behind, in frantic colors, passing.

"I hope we had fun" is the best Ned can do, standing behind her. He unties her bows. After he has unbraided her hair, he tries to braid it and then unbraids it again.

Isabel says, "You could do more than hairdressing."

But it is hard to sustain his interest here in the bare room they have found for themselves. He says, "We should do it, we should make a baby."

Poor Ned. His favorite word these days is *fuck,* though he can't do it. Fuck.

"What's the matter now?" Isabel asks. Common as a kitchen cut, her question starts a fight.

"Did I blow it?" Ned asks.

"What do you care? You were in no hurry to be liked."

"Please," Ned says. "I wasn't entirely uncharming was I?"

"No. You were very flattering about Clive's hair."

"Please."

"No," Isabel says. "I mean it."

He decides to believe her.

"What else?"

Isabel says, "You were fine."

"Turn around and tell me you mean what you just said."

Perversely, she doesn't. "Fuck off," Isabel says. "Why do you even bother getting out of bed?"

Just before she leaves the house for a walk, Isabel's manner changes with his, both of them chastened—by what? "You should come with me, Ned," she says. "Take a walk with me. It's a pretty cemetery."

No, he wants to think of pleasanter times. So does she but uglier thoughts intrude. The chocolaty laxatives she chewed after every meal—crapping over a hole in some Italian hill town while Fife and Ned drank under an awning sagged with rain. Why did her thoughts wend this way? She is here, now—look up! The oaks in the Seaside Cemetery rattle; the sky is near.

Here, with these sleepers, how easy it is to fall onto a path that should be familiar but is not. The Seaside Cemetery will never be known entirely. Today's new names are Zilpah Means and Isophene; Helen, at Rest; and Minnie. The last two are small stones. Minnie's has a rose; Helen's, nothing. Zilpah Means is buried with her husband under a twelve-foot obelisk. Isophene is all by herself, a name on a stone separated from family, a child, but whose?

Isabel's maiden name—and her professional name —is Stark. Bourne is sometimes socially expedient; thus, Dinah must think of her now as Isabel Bourne, and what is that but a foolish heart?

Speared on a pike of the wrought-iron fence are gouts of melons—watermelons—squashed troughs for flies she nears to see. Kid mischief, must be; mostly no one's here to hear the steady lobstermen at sea coughing through the fog and brushfire blue before first light every morning. Lobstermen because this is still a fishing village; but there are also—count them—three art galleries, a few bric-a-brac shops, the Trade Winds, and an older grocery that sells liquor. Across the street from the older grocery is the town hall and, up the street, the high school. Most of the town is white; the darker, waterlogged-looking places, watering holes like the Clam Box, are on the dock. A small post office—very friendly—a library, two banks, the famous Wish Nursery, two competing hardware stores, The Bay Bookstore, and the other one, for tourists, that sells puzzles and calendars and toys. A town the way a town should be, straightforward and simple as Grover's Corners with a historical society and historical sites, homesteads, deeds, seals, the picture of Amos Weed's funeral. June 1895. A windowed box of smoke on wheels, a horse-drawn summer hearse posed before the open gates of the Seaside Cemetery. The horse looks nearly dead himself though the coachman sits upright. Someone there is always brave.

★

The malign eye and the nasty snout repelled her and she couldn't set the trap. That's when Floyd and Floyd's PestGo came over—well, really, only the younger Floyd, called Pete, came over and advised against catch and release. "The darn things come back like as not": this from Pete who bent to a hole in the house. "Here's one way them squirrels get in."

Sure enough, Isabel saw this and other fissures as she followed Pete on the investigation of the Bridge House. And after Pete from Floyd and Floyd's PestGo left, she walked around the house, picking off conspicuous splinters of paint; she liked the faded yellow side of the house; the dank side, north and cold, was far less welcoming although the paint was vibrantly yellow. If the Bridge House were hers, she would paint it white: a white house made rodentless with the help of PestGo. No more acorn shards in the kitchen drawers; no more fear of finding squirrel turds in corners. When she thought of their tiny paws, she saw a bird claw, something basic that looked like a symbol of dissolution. "Am I making too much of the squirrels?"

"Yes" was Ned's answer. "You are making too much of the fucking squirrels. And you," he said, "whoever would have thought you with an exterminator?"

"I know," she said. "It's a contradiction. What can I say? Some things just don't mean as much to me. Animals with snouts, pointy faces—ferrets, minks . . ."

"And your mouse?"

"It wasn't a mouse to me."

★

For the first week, every day, Isabel drove to the long white house where Clive and Dinah lived and there modeled for Clive in his studio. Ned had seen the studio from the outside; he had not been invited in the house or entertained. Isabel had lunch with Dinah and Clive once; always she was home by early afternoon to work at the kitchen table on something of her own. "Don't ask," she said, and Ned didn't. Was it rain that kept her at the Bridge House the second week? The dining table didn't work then and she moved upstairs to the tiny bedroom with its single tiny window painted shut—stuck—she used an oscillating fan and paced the hall. Isabel did not return to Clive's studio but three or four times after the rain; after the rain—what happened? A migraine—poor woman. However, she slept; she slept somewhere else, lived on warm Coke and horse pills for headaches like hers; the smell of cooking made her sick, so Ned ate out at the Clam Box and made friends with the waitress. Well again, Isabel walked very carefully and quietly so that her head would not clatter—her word, *clatter.*

Shuuuuuush was all she said when she came back to their bed. She put her hand on his shoulder, touched his back, though they both knew by now he couldn't or wouldn't—and she?

★

She read about the greater sorrows of others caught in civil wars or genocides, their ghoulish solutions to starvation—in this book, catching small birds and biting off their heads, eating feathers, twiggy claws. The warm dead made use of. Would she, so fortunate, do anything to save herself? Shoes, blankets, warmed eggnog with brandy. The granite stoop she sat on was no longer in the sun and the air was cold off the ocean. How could she move past Rwanda to mulled wine and apples, but she was doing just that when Ned emerged from yet another afternoon spent looking too closely at the wall. She knew his disappointed face.

"What?" he asked.

"Nothing," she said. "It's getting cold out. I was about to go inside."

"I've been inside all day," he said, and he promised he would take only a short walk so they could decide on dinner.

★

The sky, Ned saw, was an ordinary blue, and the sunset was minor, and where they lived and how they lived was small. That was dinner. And after dinner more of what he was doing—small again, an essay on his mother and California and grief, for which he would be paid a modest figure. The work didn't seem worth the trouble, but he might have a memoir. He wrote after dinner, or at the least he sat in the room where he said he wrote until well past whenever Isabel had gone to bed.

She found him later on the granite stoop, look-ing out at the dark under a close sky—no moon, no shadows, cool, wet air. She went back into the house and found a blanket and brought it outside.

"Sit close," he said, and she moved closer.

Evil stories begin in basements with experiments and rats, but his own story begins under an umbrella, poolside with his mother in La Jolla. Pet, his mother, furiously ageless, looked spotty but smelled new. Empty travel, small depressions. The bent-over, boneless, sunk way she sat at the end: *I have a slight case of cancer.* His mother, poolside in La Jolla, was speaking of what would shortly kill her. Was there a dog at her feet?

Old pugs are ugly without exception—fat, gray, rumpled—and Crackle, the last of three (Snap and Pop were dead), had cataracts and farted.

They are all dead now, the dogs and Pet.

Was his mother a beauty? She must have been. Her hands at the end were translucent and barbed. He wanted to take hold of her hands and break them in his own, but he feared being cut. The sight of his own blood made him queasy, though bleeding and being bled were Pet's terms when talking about the upkeep of the La Jolla house and taxes. *I was hoping for a little comfort?*

"The blight of being conditioned for luxury without the means." Ned was quoting somebody here, but it applied to her, Ned's mother, Pet, shortened from Petronella, an old family name fished from the deep pond of a murky family, capricious and improvident. The old wheezing industrialist, his stepfather, had helped; he died before their second anniversary. Pet was left with a lot of real estate and trusts. She sold the houses—both—turned a profit, and moved to the jewel on the West Coast: lovely La Jolla. As to the trusts, she found lawyers to loosen the strings.

Infirm of purpose and very much alive, Pet had spent her last years in bed on the phone, catalog shopping, often for the dogs, ordering boxes of piddle pads for the pugs from the good doctors Foster and Smith, elastic ruffs with bells for the holidays, and treats: pig snooters for the overweight pugs. Pugs: the joke dog of the toy class, or was it nonsporting? *I love them,* his mother said. So did the Duke and Duchess of Windsor. "What can I say?"

When Isabel made no response he looked and saw she was asleep, which really didn't surprise him; at some point in the story, he was alone. The way Pet must have been alone. All night on the phone buying adorable containers and laundry baskets, shower curtains, towels, and gadgets for the grill and the garden, bud vases, doorstops, pillows to dress up the sofa, his mother readied for guests who never came. She hadn't grilled a weenie in years; everything she ate was cold and pink.

Ned had hoped for guests in Maine, for distractions, competitions, quests, ways out of the suffocating maze of memoir.

"Oh, " Isabel said, "I fell asleep." She creaked forward to stand, and the blanket fell away, and he saw the bony hanger of her shoulders and the loose way her T-shirt flapped—he can no longer remember what it was about a waif he once found attractive. Poor girl. He should hold her; he has not made such a gesture in a long time.

"Coming in?" she asked.

"Soon."

She said, "You asked me about Clive . . . before." She said, "There's nothing much between us." Whatever was it anyway but surprise and her delight at delighting an attractive man. Briefly mutual, briefly pleasurable. For her, a dinner at a restaurant with courtly pretensions and food served on fire—very festive, birthdaylike, and bewildering, but enough—better than as she is or was with Clive: on her knees between his knees whenever he pushed her into an anguished posture.

Isabel had posed for a portrait of the artist at work. Clive had put Dinah outside the studio window pulling at her garden while he worked with his back to her. "He is looking at his canvas. I'm in the foreground," Isabel said. "I'm the color of uncooked shrimp. I'm seated, curled up; my spine is exaggerated and looks like a fin. I'm a shrimp shape, no particulars at all." She said, "Everyone's face in the painting is just a suggestion."

She stood at the front door and said, "I'm not going to wait up for you."

"Don't." When she had gone, he pulled the blanket around his shoulders and hunkered down for the night. As a boy, aged eight or nine, his mother said he could sleep outside. He could sleep under the stars and as far from his house as the walled enclosure.

Once he disobeyed her and slept on the neighbors' putting green, a close-cut and cool, spongy mattress that still left its gross imprint on him. In the morning, one side of his face was stippled, red and warm against his hand.

Most golfers are like most managers: They're not very good at what they do. This, in an e-mail from Phoebe, caravanning in Scotland—where was she now? Then it was the Old Course at St. Andrew's, high-season greens fees. But where now?

Starless night, the upstairs windows were open, the hall light needlessly on. Was Isabel awake? He had put her to sleep with his story. Isabel had never met his mother; what would she have thought? Ned could hear Pet's assessment of his wife: "It doesn't look as if she can cook—that's good."

"Ned reminds me of a movie star with a few bad habits, none of them mine"—Pet talking about him in front of him. Oh, but she deplored his suspicious suits— dead men's clothes from consignment shops. She'd met Phoebe and hadn't liked her. Pet didn't have to say it—he knew, he knew, he knew, but she said it anyway: "The charm of genteel poverty wears off mighty quick." Mighty quick: Pet's tough talk. The beauty of it was Phoebe broke it off for the same reason: He did not have enough money. For his part, still true.

Ned Bourne, Edward Bourne, E. C. Bourne, Neddie. What should he call himself but what he is, a bare, dry name, Ned. On the way to their bedroom, he drags his wet finger along the wall. Where the mark he makes gives out means he will be no good for tomorrow. He hasn't enough spit. He wants to sleep. His eyes are shutting on the high season, no planted interest, no red anywhere for him but it is blunted and fecal.

★

In the morning, Ned wanted to talk.

"Let's not talk about this now," Isabel said. "Aren't you tired of it? We have two more weeks with nothing asked of us. We should be nice to each other and work." She walked away from where he sat at the edge of the bed. Downstairs in the kitchen the sensible sound of public radio put her in her place—and sure enough: another tornado in the poor flat states where so much weather seemed to happen.

The Barn
Maine, 2004

"Who was bleeding?" Dinah asked Clive. "You or me?" She had found a bloodstain, surely oral, on the sheets, but whose? Their wanton, close sleep! Most likely his, his mouth, the older, though he didn't feel any pain.

"You're welcome to look," he said, opening his mouth.

So the day came on, another day with a sky blue enough to put the sun in its place, a sky as hard to look at as the sun, although she looked up after the incongruously sweet sound of the ospreys. Straight through the afternoon she squinted and still she didn't see them until they were a dash, then out of sight. She wrote about the frog she had stared at the other day, the cold hysteria in his eyes, but frogs seemed too enervated for hysteria; they seemed lazy. The sound they made was a plucked string, the start of down-home Delta, slow. The afternoon went on and on and she worked on her geraniums—all firecracker

reds in clay pots of different sizes, some atop an old
blue box, all packed close. Maine classic. Clive was
with Isabel on the bench outside the barn; the bench,
once soldier blue, had faded to something like oyster,
a color she liked. It did not need repainting, not yet.
When the wood looked dried out and splintery then
she would paint.

But here was a change she wanted to make next
year no doubt—next year, would Isabel be in the
picture?—next year she wanted to paint the bench on
the screen porch black, eschew geraniums for a good
leaf, no blossoms necessary. A part of her was sick
of the drawn-out dying about the geraniums. From
so little a rain as a shower they seemed to emerge
sopped and spotted black and brown; they only looked
durable; their lives were short. What bewildered her
was how much she had loved them and for so long.
Her high-school sweetheart, her first love, her young
husband, James, Jimmy, Jimbo Card, a rhyme—did
he know she still loved him from time to time? Simply subdue them by loving them more was her tune.
Endure was a word in another song. She didn't always
have to be in Isabel Bourne's company; it was easier to
lunch alone. What did Ned Bourne do for lunch? She
had seen him the other day at Trade Winds shucking
ears of corn to check the kernels, shucking fast and

looking guilty about it. She had avoided him then, "glad to escape beguilement and the storm . . ." Did Robert Lowell know how much she loved him? A bit of a bully, like Clive, only madder. No, it wasn't madness in Clive, Clive wasn't mad—he was selfish, which was a fault, but a fault a person could live with. The word *endure* again. Ned Bourne squeezing avocados at Trade Winds, poking the vegetables, no, poking the meat, "and you, García Lorca, what were you doing down by the watermelons?" Patchwork poems while she waited for Clive, who had said the tide was high at four. She was ready to swim when he was and he was at four thirty, which really wasn't late. Simply subdue them by loving them more was her tune. That didn't mean she had to be in the model's company. Clive knew this much and they went to the cove alone without Isabel.

Ah! The water was a gasp and Clive swam loudly in it—a splashy stroke—while Dinah, in sunglasses, treaded in a hot spot, hung, froggylike, which was not attractive, but her aim was to stay warm with her head up and out of the water and her face dry. She was from the middle of the country; she was used to lakes and had never grown used to saltwater in her eyes. Not to say she didn't enjoy paddling in the ocean—she did—she almost didn't want to leave, so soothing was it and the air today, so cold. He promptly put a towel over her shoulders as she emerged. "Here," he said, and he put into her hand a stone he had found on the rubbly beach. The stone was bone worn and warm, not heavy, but rather light, and she turned it over in her hands, and thought of Sally, who liked to look for stones on the beach. Dinah kept them, the nicest of them, Sally's presents, on the sills of the tool shed. Now Clive was offering her a stone because, she guessed, he knew how she missed Sally. He knew she wanted company. He knew she wanted to see his daughter, but he was not up for it.

★

He pushed what Dinah had set before him away. "Why would you expect me to be sunny? I've never much liked anybody in the morning."

"I'm sorry," Dinah said, and she took up the plate of fruit she had just put before him. "How would you like your eggs?"

Dinah jiggered vodka in her juice. Vodka, blue sky, birds. Clive was almost always nicer in the afternoon. (Sally, on the telephone: "Would everyone start behaving if I had cancer?") But she had read somewhere statistics that prisoners were more likely granted parole if their hearing was in the afternoon. One explanation was people were generally happier in the afternoon.

"Sally wants to visit." This, over a late, late lunch that would serve as dinner, just the two of them, a picnic, a bully bread with a leather crust and other hard food, like salami, and iced coffee—bitter and no cream to cut it, no sugar.

"Sally wants to visit."

His response to the whistling-out-of-nowhere speed of her announcement was no response.

"She doesn't mind about the house—though it was abrupt. She just wants to see us," Dinah said. "Don't be this way. Please. Whatever it is you're fighting about . . ." Dinah hesitated because, in truth, she didn't know quite why he would not talk to Sally. Undoubtedly, the cause was trivial.

"I miss her," Dinah said. "I miss Sally."

"You shouldn't drink in the morning, Dinah. It makes you sentimental."

Sally, long ago, a large and unwashed girl on her way to camp, she needed a bra, but no one, it seemed, had told her. No one had told Sally about Dinah either; not until Clive and Dinah were married was Sally introduced to Dinah—whose idea was that? Sally's arms were shapeless even then, and the pallid skin up close was pimpled—some kind of rash. Sally's arms—most of what Dinah remembers from that time: that, and her impulse to hug the girl. Stepdaughter? The word was too harsh for such a big, gentle soul.

"You talk about Sally as if she were a Saint Bernard."

"Oh, Clive, please!"

Sally stretched out along the picnic cloth was long, nearly as tall as Clive—six feet—and her backside, monumental.

"I know Sally can be needy, has been—is!" Dinah didn't want to yell. Who was she to scold?

When Dinah woke from her nap, she saw the meadow had been mown. The fieldstones were visible again. They looked like lumpish animals in the muddy embankment, and Clive, at the shed, appraising, seemed pleased—pleased with the appearance of everything, himself included, and why not? The smooth movable parts of him—nothing caved in or stiff or dry about Clive, nothing barreled but his chest was russet colored, ardent—all worked, and the whole of him turned to her now, welcoming. Up close, he smelled grassy. Was it any wonder what she did, what she had done, and would do again for the attentions of this man? Years ago Dinah had left the young husband—known long but married shortly—for this man, Clive Harris, older but not by so many years anymore. Left a husband, a hometown, and friends for a man who openly cheated on her even then. Oh, pride was overrated; she had learned how to put it aside. Drinking a little helped and the days when she fancied she had written a good line, which sometimes turned into a poem and a good one at that.

"Does the meadow meet with your approval?" Clive asked, and in asking she knew he was sorry, sorry about Sally. He was sorry but he did not want to talk about his daughter. No more about Sally, please. No more, and they turned back to the long white house with the wind dropped to nothing and the wind chimes quiet.

★

At some unrecognizable hour, Dinah woke to his juddering hand. He was turned away, but the movement he made, his seeming light, expert touch impressed her, and Dinah tugged at herself a little, but hard so it hurt, which was a way to feeling, and she went off to sleep thinking about her age—sixty—and Clive's age and Sally's. The Bournes, how old were they? Ned

Bourne was in her dream, ineffective, silent, seated, yet comely compared to the woman she saw or what might have been a woman: Where there should have been breasts were cavities; where hair, a coarse whorl, a black twat.

"Oh, what a terrible dream I had!" were her first words in the morning.

He didn't ask her to recount it, but she would not have told him; no more than she would tell him that she, too, often cried in the morning—what remedy? She had her jiggered-up juice from time to time and reveries of children. She was sorry she had not prevailed on the subject of children. Childlessness was a hole in her life, and how a child might map this house was a game she had played for years—still did. By what surfaces, what smells, colors, places, dogs would a child know this house?

Something Sally did one summer when she stayed with them in Maine. She was old enough to drive by then, but didn't; rather, every morning, she and Clive set themselves up—he seated in a wheelbarrow en plein air. Sally had a foldout chair but stood, even then, restless or jumpy, a girl who trembled to be spoken to though her hand was steady. The watercolors Sally made were as precise as oils. Dinah had one, a painting of stalks and tassels, high summer greens; she hung it in the sunny nest where she wrote in the winter—a green memory of summer.

Which of the daylilies would a granddaughter favor? The cream-colored, ruffled 'Longfield's Beauty' or the velvety red 'Woman's Work'? The yellows will not move her—and 'Going Bananas' is just another yellow, but the name might win her over. Dinah didn't like the common orange when she was a kid, so why should a granddaughter, fancifully made, embrace them? (Poor Wisia is not fancifully made. She hasn't the attention span for flowers. She likes camp and archery—and may come to love horses.) Go on with the game, and Dinah does, thinking a granddaughter has come to visit. The stone floor in the kitchen is cold underfoot in the morning and Grandfather is a grump, but Grandmother wears an apron—hug her!—she is bacony and sweet.

Dinah would like to tell Clive that she wants grandchildren, that the unaccountably odd Wisia is preferable to silence, and Sally is his daughter.

★

"Let's start the morning over again," she said. "How do you want your eggs?"

★

After the smear of lunch, blue skies and a chance to play with watercolors, sleep, no swimming today but she was caught up in the cocktail hour and playing around with the festive mesclun, washed red bits sticking to her hands—"My day?" Dinah considered. "It was," and she tossed the salad not unhappily though she heard his knuckle-crackling sounds and sighs.

"Break the seal on the whiskey," he said, and she turned away from the sink to do it. Five Motrim at a swack usually did the trick for him, but tonight the ache went on. He was looking at his feet.

"Your drink," she said, and now she looked at his feet and was awed by the crisscrossed, ropy varicosities knotted at his ankles. Was it any wonder he ached?

★

"Good morning, sweetheart!" Clive was not always glum. So why did she ruin the day with mention of Sally?

"I'm not talking about the Bournes," she said. "Why can't Sally stay with us?"

"I saw a lot of Sally in New York this spring. Too much of Sally," he said. "I don't want to go on outings to Isle au Haut." Clive said, "I want to work," and his purpose was as final as a nail.

Once your parents die, there is nothing between you and it. Not a new idea, but the reality has pressed against his heart. Clive has had his mother on his mind. And not because Ned Bourne has made it his subject—no, hardly that; rather, remorse over his own behavior toward the women in his life has Clive facing backward to where his mother left off. Would she approve? Doubtful. *Your father would never* was how she reprimanded Clive when he was growing up. He sees his mother from a distance and then spends the night by her side. His mother in imposing diamonds at the Hotel Gritti, New Year's Eve, the passing of the year in which his father had died, Clive sat with his mother while she delivered her pronouncements on Daddy's genius, his kindness, his elegance—such assertions had hissed past his ears before, chiding; but on this one night she spoke of his father's gift for life and for loving others. "Your father was a man who let things go alive."

Then with the alacrity of another new year, she tucked the dead man into her clutch, quoting him only from time to time when it served instructive. Scolding Sally's table manners, "Your grandfather used to say only boiled and roasted joints allowed on the table!"

Clive thinks his mother liked to poke Sally in the elbow with a fork. In this way Clive thinks he is more like his mother: He's a killer.

The other day he had told Isabel he would not be needing her services for a while. Poor choice of words, probably, but he was not given to lying. He had told her from the start, just as he had once told Dinah, he must have full sway.

★

"I told you. Clive's on to the lily pond," Isabel said.

"I'm sorry," Ned said.

"Whatever for?"

Advancing across the sky, clouds promised a storm of Olympian proportion. The power might go out. Now something appropriately dramatic would happen.

Ned wanted to know, "Should we get buckets?"

"Does the roof leak?"

(The weather that time with the dying mouse when Ben stood behind a grill big enough to roast a boar and Phoebe whisked the dressing, the weather then had been threatening but nothing came of it until the next morning when they drove back to New York in a downpour. Rain on a Sunday—all very appropriate.)

She asked, "Should I feel sorry for you?"

He made some helpless gesture—as if a sale had not gone through or he was broke or lost, unable to answer. "Yes, no, I don't know." He tried to explain to her—as much as to himself—that Phoebe was making her summer rounds, visiting her father and her stepmother, her stepfather and her mother, and Ben's mother and father. Part of Phoebe's vacation was being spent on different family compounds, another part was offbeat Europe with well-traveled friends. How did he feel about this, Isabel wanted to know. "Do you want to figure more prominently in her life?"

Just when they were on to an important topic, the phone rang and she knew it was Clive. Before Ned even spoke, she knew from his expression of complicit exasperation that Clive had asked Ned if he might speak to her. "No," Ned said, delightedly. Ned looked at Isabel and lied about her whereabouts, and all the time he was talking, Isabel didn't signal for the phone, but watched Ned and wondered why he was so sure this was what she wanted him to do—when she didn't know what she wanted Ned to do—or Clive to do, for that matter.

"Thanks a lot," she said.

"I really didn't think you'd want to speak to him. I'm sorry," Ned said, and he sounded quite genuinely sorry; it made her sorry, sorrier, and sadder.

"It's all right," she said. "I didn't want to speak to him." But she wasn't sure if what she said was true. She was also thinking of Phoebe.

"Now that we're in Maine," Ned began, "it might be fun . . . ," but he had no need of finishing when he saw Isabel's expression—God knows he wanted to be hopeful himself. "We should read *The Odyssey* together. The epic belongs to beautiful women—Odysseus visits the underworld and is witness to a parade of them, a great loveliness of ghosts with stories of ravishment, fleet sons, and sorrow."

★

The barn is preternaturally white before the storm; her warm sides heave, bovine and alive, patient. Clive gestures toward the house and Dinah moves. She feels afraid of the storm but also dreamy. The grass is very green and squeaks underfoot, and all the while Clive is nudging her forward to the house and up the stairs. Love! She is also afraid. How she must look: the dull hair, her hair, all this way and that, flat patches, a child's morning hairdo, the nut-size skull, and the scalp that shows through. Terrible thoughts when he means only to please her. And she is pleased and feels purely lucky to be touched.

"Why are you crying?" Clive asks.

"Any number of reasons."

"I'll squeeze it out of you, whatever it is," Clive says.

In Transit
2004

All night sentimental voices in a continuous loop of sound played in the airport. "I should know," Sally shouted at the little phone in her hand. Cell phones, she hated them. "Can you hear me, Dinah? Yes?" She pressed a button along the side of the phone. "This any better?" Sally asked. "I can hear you better." Shut down by a storm and being cheap, Sally had spent the night in the Boise airport. Now she watched a half-assed sunrise turn the sky white and perceived no change in the lounge. She was alone; she was alone in the airport but for a man in a red shirt on the other side of the security gate near the end of a spooky job; the concessions stands—two to be exact— were gated. No CAUTION signs, no woman swabbing the tunneling entrance to the women's restroom, so Sally held it in, wouldn't go, endured the knotted sensations because who was to say? Murderers—the man in the red shirt, someone she had missed in the long night in the empty airport where the escalator still kept running—ghostly.

The escalator and the music! The music was a threaded needle working its way through her brain.

"Oh, Sally." Dinah spoke softly into the phone, fearful lest she wake Clive sleeping next to her in bed.

"What am I punishing myself for? I could have stayed at a motel."

"Sally."

"Some of the money from the painting Dad gave me went to this camp, you know."

"Sally . . ."

"I loved horses at her age. They always took advantage of me but I loved them." Sally returned to the airport experience and her good fortune in having a book to read.

But Wisia on a horse was on Dinah's mind.

Sally said, "I actually finished this book. It got me through the long night. I've underlined pages—here." Sally put on her reading voice, the one she wore with glasses: "'Encaustic images of women in funerary portraits were discovered in the nineteenth century at Fayum in Egypt.' That's nice to know, isn't it?"

"I thought you said the book was about jigsaw puzzles. What does that have to do with jigsaw puzzles?"

"A lot," Sally said. "Margaret Drabble makes it fit. She is so smart and frugal. She doesn't like taking taxis. Art, family, old age. Dad would like it."

"Oh, Sally."

"I'm coming to you, Dinah," she said. "I don't care what Dad says."

"Did you have any dinner at all last night?"

"I kicked an old Baby Ruth out of the vending machine. The peanuts were white. Bad sign. But I had no choice; Sabarro's was shut up. The drinks in the vending machine looked like cleaning fluid." Sally said, "The meal they'll be serving in the next life."

"I don't know why you didn't go to a motel."

"I did expect the lights to dim."

Instead there was music and CNN. All night the breaking news scrolled across the TV along with footage of the killer whale who had killed his trainer: the killer whale corkscrewing into the air, breaking the water with his tail or else sliding up a ramp, his expression disingenuously smiley. "He had a history of violence," Sally said.

"No," Dinah said softly into the phone, no, she had not seen the killer whale.

"I had to pee something terrible," Sally said. "Fortunately people started to return to the airport a little while ago. I'm a go."

Clive cued Dinah to whisper, so she whispered in a rush for Sally not to drive if she was tired.

"I'm in the airport, Dinah. I'm flying."

★

The morning! It began again, real delight at Clive close in bed. "Don't get up just yet," he said. She let him knead her back and her neck and her arms, and she thanked her good fortune until the phone. "Damn it," Clive said, though it was Dinah who sat up and answered.

The voice was Isabel's, not Sally's.

"What time is it now?" Dinah asked. Long past morning, past expectation and nearer dread. Dinah was sorry to say she had not seen Ned; she was especially sorry when she learned that he was not supposed to drive, that he had lost his license a few months ago; moreover, that he was under medication. *I understand,* Dinah said, although she didn't quite understand the meandering account of Ned and the medicine he took; Dinah didn't quite understand the sequence of events either—how the young couple went from the afternoon through the evening. "Gone since when?" Dinah hoped to hear something more specific than "sometime in the night." Isabel couldn't be sure. She simply woke to discover Ned missing and the car gone.

"How sad," Dinah said, first to Isabel and then, hanging up the phone, to Clive. "Oh, pity the wives, 'their brief goes straight up to heaven and nothing more is heard of it.'"

"That's good," he said. "What's happened?"

Dinah told him what she knew. "I hope he didn't drive in the storm."

"He slept in the car, I'll bet," Clive said. "Are you up for good now?"

And in truth, Dinah didn't know, but she slapped the hairbrush around her head. No matter there wasn't much of it, hair came first in the construction of her face.

"So I take it that's the end of our morning?"

"Oh, God," she said. "This doesn't happen every day." She saw the blazoned grizzle on his chest and his loose old arms, still muscled, still powerful, and she was moved, and put her hairbrush aside and went back to bed. His hair—there was so much of it, a silvery white, no yellow in it, and his eyebrows, darker. They moved when he talked, which was rarely, but Ned Bourne . . . Ned, why did he have to come into her story all of a sudden?

★

The cheap princess phone looked like a giant aspirin, the oblong kind. "Fuck me. Fuck me to shit fuck shit!" The phone scratched in her ear and the ring lacked conviction. "Answer this time, you fuck. Answer." But the first time she called, Dinah said hello. Oh, fuck. Isabel, stumbling through her story, considered the frenzied appearance of the house behind her: rag rugs skidded in her pratfall search for him—Ned? Closet door opened. Ned? By the time she made the second call, Isabel had straightened the house—nothing tippy or off—and she was lucky this time: Clive answered.

"Can you hear me?"

"Can you hear me?"

"Yes, yes I can," she said, and she threw herself into her sorrows: "Ned was just so nice to me for the first time in a long time. We talked."

"Why do you think he left?"

"I don't know."

"Don't cry."

"Why ever did you think I'd be happier here?"

"I don't know," he said. "Maybe if you'd come alone."

"Even so," she said. "This is your daughter's house."

"My house," he said.

Isabel said, "It needs work." All she had to do was lift the tatty skirt to the apron-front sink to be assaulted by the basement gloom of old pipes and a floor that looked tarred. "You should visit," she said, and when he didn't answer, Isabel told him about the Electrolux in the closet. "Vintage fifties," she said, "easy."

"Why did you?" she said, accusing, not asking.

"Sorry?"

"What was I thinking coming here?"

"Isabel."

"Why don't you love me?" she asked, and when he didn't answer, she said, "It doesn't matter," and she pulled out the cord for the whiplashed finish, the big bang of nothing before she shoved the princess phone in yet another empty drawer. It rarely rang. Old house, the Bridge House, and the path to the other house, Clive's house, was not quite as he had described it—no mown swath of lawn from one stoop to the other but houses out of sight of each other parted by land as hard as heath, a plaid field—fall-like—blocks of piney woods, another field with a mown path to Clive's house, nameless, long and white. To walk from one house to the other was not to be undertaken lightly. In the plaid field, thorns scored the body and stung; nothing drooped but stood up in the heat—and today, huzzah! The out-of-doors roughly washed, not yet dry but cooler, cleaner, like walking through sheets on a clothesline. Down the hill across the road she went to where the incline toward the coast began steeply. Wild roses, pink scraps of color, sweet-smelling but hairy stemmed, full of prickers, hedged a narrow path to the rusty-colored stratum, the coast's outcroppings that in the light looked holy but inspired thoughts of soft things bashed against them. (She had a plate in her hand.)

★

He must have walked—Dinah's first conjecture when she saw him. There was an uncertain path, but a path, from the forest through the field to where the apple trees started and the lawn was nubbled, scant, mown, the chicken coop now a studio for Dinah to work in, and nearby the tool and potting shed for Dinah's garden. The garden itself was delicately fenced, an illusion of nets in trellises and curly vines, broken vines—a boggy odor—tomato and squash; beyond that, nibbles of lettuce, mostly dirt and not so soaked, but its hard crust was white in the sun. Already! The young man must have walked from the village. What was it about this boy, the newly arrived Ned Bourne, that held her attention? For one, he was Isabel Bourne's husband, and she wondered how a man handsomer than Rossetti could have failed his wife? Or she failed him? She imagined his days, dragging in to dinner, sickened by the ort of breakfast floating in the sink and nothing made. There may be cures to loneliness but marriage is not one of them. Dinah had a garden and makeup and a tipsy habit—she had friends on the side. Poems? They grew.

Oh, why were the young so slow to turn to life when they had it? The handsome Ned Bourne from her window, Ned Bourne, seated on the bench, leaned back against the barn and looked up unwashed and overheated, open mouthed, yet handsome, drinking the cure of Clive's attentions. He must have taken the highway, then cut through the woods the last two miles and across the field to the barn by foot. Barefoot, quietly arrived, scratched up, grubby, bloody, Ned Bourne, it seemed, had walked from the village.

If someone were to ask her was she still in love with Clive, Dinah would say, "Yes, very much so, decidedly." It would not surprise her if Ned Bourne should come to love him—Dinah had seen Clive's students brighten in his company, and she had watched the willing girls, too, one most unsteady from UT where Clive was a visiting professor. (Isabel Bourne didn't seem so unsteady as sad. "I am not turning into the person I wanted to be" was what Isabel had said, a little drunkenly, sweetly, the night they parted company at the Clam Box.) The girl from UT wore jeans and English riding boots and tops that seemed as slight as scarves or made of scarves, a summery way about them, as sheer as curtains, lifting in a small breeze. The girl had no breasts to speak of. What was her name? Emma, Lynne, Lou? She asked intelligent questions although Dinah had heard such questions and their answers before, so that she dared to leave them, this Emma girl and Clive, to bob, in her fashion, in the pool. The pool was a part of the faculty complex—a hushed place, washed and planted and tended to by Mexicans. The sprinkler system spurted on at night. Not without surprise and certainly delight, Dinah remembers how she left them, walking bravely into unmitigated light— the blue square of water against pink verticals—she left them alone in a cool room, Clive and this girl, the sloppy human element, and Dinah did not look back. So now, why not guests? Why not Sally—on her way? And Ned? Ned, come from the village and the Clam Box, no doubt, but come in the spirit of one invited. Guests, of course, yes, even in sleep Dinah had heard Clive thrusting the lawnmower this way and that; a mown path, what was it but an invitation?

★

Clive watched Ned Bourne's hair dry as they sat together on the bench outside the barn. The strands dried singly—red, brown, black, yellow—softened, blended, waved. From where had he come and why at this hour? At some point Clive told Ned that he should do whatever he had to do. (Clive later regretted this advice when he learned Ned was speaking of Phoebe. Phoebe of Phoebe and Ben—Ben was his nephew, for Christ's sake!)

Ned told Clive that he had walked to the barn from the village because he did not dare drive home. "I lost my license," Ned said, "but I drove to the Clam Box last night." So the story came out, he went to see the girl—two girls, it turned out; a duller friend tagged along—the waitress he had noticed on the night he first met Clive.

"Do you know the waitress I'm talking about? She has a lot of hair?"

Clive suspected it was Ellie but he would not say.

Ned shrugged.

Clive was sure it was Ellie, Ellie Phlor, whose thoughts came out the size of beads strung together with *like, like, like, like never, like what the*? Ellie Phlor was rumored articulate in other ways.

"No," Clive said, "no idea."

The bench on this side of the barn was in the shade, and the grass there still wet enough for Ned to wash his feet in it. "What's the time, anyway?" he asked.

"Not sure," Clive said, "near noon?"

Ned lifted himself off the bench and followed Clive to the back porch, where he sighed to sit again.

"I didn't think your house was so far from town."

"No one offered you a ride?"

"There were not so many cars on the road. It was late," he said.

"You look as if you might fall asleep."

"I might."

Sunday, midmorning, very quiet but for that shrill insect sound of old, the whistle of childhood's high summer, that sound heard once, twice, then Dinah arrived with drab yellow drinks that worked miracles.

Dinah said, "What if the hokey pokey really is what it's all about?" She touched Clive's shoulder, saying not to worry, mostly lemonade.

"Whatever you've mixed, I feel better already," Ned said.

★

Overbleached, Dinah's hair shocked around her head inspiring tenderness in Clive as he attended the sad case of the handsome Ned Bourne, whose eyes were closed—poor bastard. The spectacle of the Bournes. He phoned Isabel to tell her that Ned was with them on the porch, but when he heard a busy signal, Clive grew angry. All of a morning ruined—or nearly. Back on the porch, he saw Dinah ministering to Bourne; she had his feet in a pan of warm water and Epsom salts.

"He's resting his eyes," Dinah said, "which is good."

For a moment, he thought he might work, but then Dinah told him about Sally and the airport and the storm, bigger than last night's rain, that was still on its way to them. And Sally was on her way, too.

"I knew it," he said.

"I like her company, Clive, very much. I like women."

★

Ned, dreamy, was making his way across a room of shirtfronts and bare arms. He was looking for Isabel, who had disappeared. Somewhere in the crowded room of dressy people, most of them his age, was his wife. I am looking for my wife. I am looking for Isabel; but there was the crone again, the old witch with the mustache. Damn it. He startled awake in a wicker chair on an empty porch. His feet felt powdered, and when he looked down, it seemed to him they glowed opalescent. *Epsom salts,* the sound of the words was soothing until he remembered where he was and the way he had walked the seven miles from town to Clive's barn. He must have started the car, then smartly thought better of it: Safer to walk, but how did he lose his shoes? He banged his pockets for keys or a wallet—nothing.

They had left him sleeping on the porch. The house was still and he was alone, but feeling healed, able to walk home. He made a soft exit and walked on the grassy verge of the road. Had he put his hand on the halo of Dinah's head? Had he kissed Clive? They seem to have disappeared if ever they were there. The soundless bay was a gray line beyond a grayer shoreline; the sky was growing wider. Here in the company of large elements Ned felt how it must be for Isabel with him. Pitchforked treachery on a bonfired night, and she, in the midst of it, insubstantially dressed.

"I'm sorry," he said when he saw her.

★

Standing in the yard at the back of the house, not so much a yard at all but long grasses, field asters—what some call weeds—Isabel pulled her hand up the long stems to things and took off the leaves until her hand, stained, hurt and smelled smoky.

"I understand," she said, "if we'd spent the summer apart maybe."

"Who knows?"

"That was the plan," she said.

"For you, maybe."

"With you, I don't know, I don't know if I can, I have ambitions, you know, I . . . ," she faltered, ashamed, unable to say what she wanted to be and silenced by a familiar expression of his—a broil of hurt and suspicion. Who was to say what anyone might make of a life, but Isabel was stung by the little startles of those who knew her at what she had become. From the girl most promising—no book, no significant publications either, and online didn't count. She kept a journal; but she had not been a success, except perhaps outwardly in marriage. And now the marriage was over.

★

"I'm sorry," Ned said again when he came downstairs with a packed bag and his computer. He had thought as she had thought, but why comb through expectations? Theirs, a short romance, three years if Columbia counted, no more than a sniffle, an accumulation of scenes in thrift shops and workshops, a whimsical wedding in a rhinestone casino. *I will if you will yes.* Las Vegas, 2002. Road trip in his late mother's car—the Solaris convertible, cherry red. (Do the really rich own cars in bright colors? Her father's Mercedes was silver and scdate.) Ned's mother had wanted to keep her Mercedes. "I can't keep up with the upkeep": Pet's joke. She was already sick, so why not trade in for an optimistic car and find someone to drive her? The housekeeper's husband, of course!

The hungry eye followed by the numb, dumb discovery Ned made at the little there was to remember, and nothing that others hadn't already known. Some images repeated: His mother, in shades of yellow, orchidaceous, was in love with the royals. ("That poor maligned duchess!" Pet said.) Their crests, their pugs, their cigarettes. Weak light with fog bank for background, Pet, in velvet slippers and round tortoise-shell sunglasses, sipped coffee at the umbrella table. The umbrella was furled, the blue pool, pale; nature for Ned was just bushes and flowers.

"Don't cry," he said before he saw Isabel's expression. Most of the big cries, as she called them, had happened on the road, at hotels, motels—weeks ago in the Wax Hill B & B on their way to Clive and the Bridge House. In the B & B they had suffered all night in a white box because, uninvited as he was, she wanted Ned at the Bridge House if it meant he was giving up Phoebe. Then she could concentrate, if she knew he had given up Phoebe. He had hoped to.

And as to Clive, what was she to him but a different shape to paint?

Ned said Isabel *was* more than to paint. He turned away and once in the drive looked back again at her wide-open face: It was made for wonder. Straight, finger-thick eyebrows, gray eyes, soft expression, Isabel.

"Good-bye," he said.

She seemed unmoved to see him go, said, "Thanks for leaving me the car." And a dun-colored cab came slyly out of the fog and up the drive. Ned approached with a thuggish duffel bag. The trunk popped up, and the driver emerged, a shapeless man—two eyes, a nose, somewhere a mouth—distinctive as a carrot, gone hairy, limply aged. He fit the occasion, self-described as from the county, that northern bareness, seeming flat but for Katahdin on the map. Fog was nothing to a man from Aroostook used to much worse; whereas Ned, Ned was from a softer part of the country and bound for an even softer place: Bermuda of the pretty clichés—pink sands, turquoise waters. Phoebe had said hurricane season is best for lots of reasons.

Honestly!

Her voice in his ear's a hoarseness he loves to hear. That and her money was why she got away with everything.

★

"Do you remember that first summer when Sally locked herself in her room every night, and the door stuck? It wouldn't shut for her to lock it. I had to push from the other side."

"I don't know why you'd want to remember," Clive said, "and you're smiling."

But she had liked that noisy, nighttime business.

On Sunday afternoons, Dinah's grandfather let the Newfies lie near the fire in the den and watch old Westerns with him. Dinah said, "Whenever one of the dogs farted, and it was almost always Tom, my grandfather lit a match."

Dinah said, "Sally had nothing to be afraid of then."

"Her mother was living with that man."

"Sally should get a dog."

Clive said, "She has Wisia."

But only in the summers and six weeks of this one at camp—and that was money well spent. Dinah had seen the girl kick Sally in a most hurtful place, stood witness, helpless to part them—afraid really. Wisia was more respectful of her other mother and why was that?

Dinah said, "Sally's driving up from Portland."

"You amaze me," Clive said.

"I'm glad," she said. For Sally's sake, she hoped the Bournes would both vacate although she felt maternally toward them, felt other stirrings, too, and sadness.

The Bridge House
Maine, 2004

The knock on the door was the loose door itself in the wind, and Isabel kept her eyes shut and her face in the sun. The door in the wind, in the wind and the pitched light of late afternoon in the backyard, she saw where she was and, too, for an instant, a not so tall man stretched out on the bulkhead: Ned of the slender ankles, shapely leg. Too handsome.

His story always started with *I was invited to this* . . .

Isabel shut her eyes and listened for a voice, a word more, which, when it came, came from a woman. Woman? Women?

On the kitchen table near the open windows was a tiny bottle of fluttery sweet peas feigning faint of heart. A note, too, but Isabel didn't move to get it. The Bridge House was not reliable.

Stupid.

The Bridge House, 1858, yellow clapboard, the yellow almost all worn away. Old trees. Old windows, wiggly glass. No bridge figured into it; the first owner's name was Gray, and after him, a spinster daughter, Margaret. Occupied for more than a hundred years by the same family, a New England farmhouse not so far from the road, a winter house, austere and brave, high elevation, hard on a hill overlooking the bay! The bay and, but for Mr. Weed and his establishment, open meadow, pines, outcroppings. But Mr. Weed, the menacing Mr. Weed, lived at the bend in the road in a warren of outbuildings, where he serviced lawn mowers, sold parts. She had introduced herself—she had seen the photo of his ancestor and seen his ancestors' graves at the Seaside Cemetery. Mr. Weed was on his knees and too old to get up quickly.

"Please don't!" she had said even as he stood.

On clear days Isabel could see Acadia in the distance.

★

Sally said to her father, "You think I'm staying forever. I know what you're thinking."

"You do, do you?" Clive asked.

Dinah was out of the door with her arms open, bumping past him and into the cushion of Sally in slacks. Dinah, no bigger than a darning needle, put her arms around Sally's waist and hugged, exuberant. As long as they keep it to themselves, why shouldn't he suffer his daughter's visit? Dinah wanted company, whereas he was no sooner in company than he wanted to be out of it and back in the barn. Not that he was always productive, Christ, no. A lot of looking went into what he was doing. For a time he had liked to look at Isabel, bony as she was, but he was looking elsewhere now. A fox, a fox and her kits, had come upon him from time to time when he had set up in the field to paint early in the morning, and he was smitten. Mama fox, lighthearted in the high grass, when her focus turned on him, she held still; she stood self-possessed and cool and looked right through him. Mama fox. The kits were merely foolish.

"I'm happy to see you, too, Dad," Sally said and she made an affectionate move toward him as she dragged what looked like camping gear behind her.

"Smells syrupy in here. Did you make waffles this morning, Dinah?"

Had she? He didn't remember. "No one tells me anything," Clive said, more to himself than to anyone

listening, moving out of the kitchen to the back porch.
Dinah already at the disaster site, saying, "Shared cus-
tody is often not shared." He wished there were some
other story. People were moving about him even as
he moved away. Dinah, last glimpsed with branches
of weigela in a Ball jar. He remembered that part of
breakfast at least.

★

The last corner before the last so sharply inclined to the
shore that Ned's car, now Isabel's car, fishtailed off the
road—an accident! The tree broke the car's fall, or who
knows how far down the hill she might have gone.
Isabel was unhurt, but when she dared to see how far
down was down, she got sick. And this fuck-up after all
she had accomplished in asking Mr. Weed to help her
get her car—on Pearl near the Clam Box, where else?
She must have forgotten she was driving or something
equally stupid—a dumb accident might explain her
accident. Embarrassed, wiping her mouth, not quite
relieved. The back window of the car was a blown-
out sheet of glass—green diamond edges beguiling
as a gemstone. The back door was dented, half-open.
Otherwise the car worked.

"My God!"

The policeman did not remind her of any person in authority.

"It was so easy," she said, "in slow motion and so much damage, but I'm all right, thank you, really. That such a tiny accident should cause so much damage. The car's worth nothing now, I guess. Not even trade-in. Scrap."

Once home, she sat on the granite step looking out at the bay. It took a while before the sensation of falling ceased.

She talked to her mother for a time and was comforted by her terrorized reaction. "Why?" Her mother said, "You have to ask me why I'm so upset? After this whole shameful business . . ." The sentence was abandoned. "Please," her mother said, "if it's about Ned, I don't want to know."

★

"Ned was hoping for guests," Isabel said when Dinah and Sally arrived. "We've got rum and vodka, gin, six or seven bottles of modest house red. I'm leaving it here with you, if that's okay."

"No," Sally said. "Don't you want it?"

"I'll take it," Dinah said, "but Isabel don't drive back to New York right away, at least stay through the weekend."

"I hadn't planned staying longer," Isabel said. She thanked them for the surprise of the sweet peas, and then she was crying. She was crying, and Dinah and Sally led her out of the kitchen into a front room with sun. They sat on either side of her on the sofa.

They didn't know about the car. Clive had not told them, but they wanted to know, animated by talk about accidents with machines and people: the surprising force of slight collisions and accident lore. How once, Dinah remembered, a not-so-large tree limb overloaded with wet snow fell on the tool shed and crushed it.

The usual disaster commiserations brought the women together: They had all dinged some car, lost keys, forgotten gas; they had surprised themselves with their own fragility: falling on a street, banging into something with an edge. Tables!

"I don't remember there being so little furniture," Sally said, "but you put in new screens?"

"No," Dinah said. "I sent Nan Black to clean before Isabel . . ."

Isabel was apologizing for the mess. She planned on cleaning as soon as she knew what she was doing;

she was weepy about the car, the shock and expense of it, and then she was speaking about Ned: How often she had heard herself asking, "But you're not a fuck, are you?" And his answering, "Yes, I am."

Isabel said, "Dinah, I'm so sorry."

"I know," Dinah said, and she looked around the room and appeared delighted and surprised at her own foresight: "I sent Nan."

"New screens?" Sally asked.

"Just Nan, Nan Black."

"It's so bright," Sally said. "I don't remember its being so bright."

Isabel pushed herself out from the couch, saying, "I've been throwing away a lot of Ned's crap." Why did she always pick mean words? "Some clothes are nice and a few books."

"Don't give away his books," Dinah said. "He should have them."

The three women on the stairs—Sally held the banister as if it were the handle to a suitcase—ostensibly to look over whatever Isabel had labeled nice. At the landing, Isabel watched as what seemed dank and threatening, oppressively wallpapered on the sunless side of the house dried, darkened, and turned softly old in Dinah's company. The wide-board floors painted gray were smooth enough to walk on barefoot, but Isabel was in the habit of slipping off her slippers at the edge of the bed and otherwise wearing them. Now she saw what Clive meant but Sally wasn't too tall for the Bridge House. She walked through the house comfortably, seeming happy in the fact that the house worked: Lights, door handles, locks; room to room she walked until she reached the room Ned had seized to work in—and why not? No one ever said he wasn't selfish. Isabel stood with Sally and Dinah at the opened windows. The clamorous brilliancy of the bay was not tamed even at this distance from this height. The height made Isabel dizzy and she stepped back just as Sally sat on the table, the same Ned used for work. "Ah, hah!" Sally said. "Where the magic happens?" and she used her arm as a dust rag over the powdered surface. "Was he working here?" Sally asked.

The house faltered. "I thought," Isabel said, and she steadied herself on the desk edge and wondered that the time Ned had spent in this wide room with all its light should yield up the parts he had read her, indulgences, lugubrious and trite—except that Carol Bane had approved. In consideration of events in the world the only noble calling was to report on them. Where were the orphans in Ned's work but he was sitting under an umbrella table with a silly woman feeding table scraps to dogs? What did a person say to such audacity as Ned's? To write a memoir didn't a person have to suffer a little?

Sweet Neddie, he seemed so, seemed so _____. Fill in the blank. Blank? Ned was on his way to Bermuda —he had told her as much.

Sally was talking about the view while Dinah was opening closets, saying, "I'm told there's an old Electrolux somewhere?"

"I'm going to let you look around," Isabel said to the women, for which they both apologized, looking around.

"I haven't seen the house since Dad bought it," Sally said.

Dad, Isabel heard, and she thought, *Clive,* and she saw that the woman uttering the word *Dad* was her age, and she was ill at ease again. "I'll be in the back outside," Isabel said. "Take your time," she said, but whose house was this? What house? The Bridge House was unstable and teetering.

When had this started?

Weeks ago: She had seen the front door of the Bridge House open onto the ocean, and in the distance a small boat, tinier and plainer than Brueghel's, was moving away equally indifferent to Isabel's dilemma: how to get out of the Bridge House? Even out of the house, she felt endangered, which was stupid. She was safe indoors and out. The sea was nowhere near. Nothing was tilted but her vision of Ned, lying on the backyard bulkhead to the cellar, head tipped back, eyes shut, sculpted throat sacrificially thrust forward. The backyard was wildly untended, full of high danger. Here in the backyard was where he told her he was sorry, he felt it was best, he knew now, he was leaving. Phoebe! Phoebe! Phoebe! *As You Like It* was a violent comedy, though the last time she saw it, she had cried when old Adam died onstage, reverenced at the fire by the banished duke's men.

The reward of long service is no more service.

But on to other considerations. Will Ben Harris catch up to his quick-witted wife? Of everyone involved she felt sorriest for Ben—no, she felt sorriest for herself.

★

After Sally and Dinah had gone, putting dibs on nothing, all of it crap, Isabel stood near a closet holding on to the sleeve of Ned's shirt. A terrible stillness in her ears, some empty sound.

Only weeks ago, she had driven to a deserted house off the Reach Road and there had broken what windows in the house were left to break.

Ned had said he didn't know what it was about her but he did not find her sexy. Maybe it was her clothes. She was so often in doubt.

"What clothes?"

"My point," he said. "Exactly."

How nasty it seemed now that he should have criticized her wardrobe. Isabel in the Bridge House packed up Ned's clothes; a slouchy, dirt-colored sweater she kept. He hadn't left much behind. The long socks knotted in his sock drawer she threw away. Anything with a netted interior, of course, was also out. Haha.

In the last week she had told him that his penis was small.

That his penis was small, he knew; but her cunt, he said, was enormous.

In whatever game it was they played, Ned and Isabel had made a point of staying even.

"You want me to pay attention," Ned said, "I know. I'm trying."

She curled his belt in a shoe box for charity, but his hairbrush she kept for his smell.

Why do that?

How could she explain herself to herself or to anyone? Both of them from elsewhere, they had lived

in different cities. New York, the longest. Columbia
first, West Ninety-eighth, later the White Street loft.
Left unused, the White Street loft was an overturned
fishbowl: unwashed windows in punishing southern
light. Caught air—terrible—but now, night after night,
to put herself to sleep, she passed through the White
Street loft swiping her hand over onyx edges and surfaces that started liquidy and cool, then turned solid.
The hard immovables: column, sill, headboard. Hard
headboard, yes, built-in and recessed. Was that possible
and was it possible in just a summer to forget? Isabel
walked down the long hall past the La Jolla scenes, large
black-and-white photographs of Ned and his mother,
Pet, and so to sleep, but the Bridge House roused her,
a sound.

"Who's here?"

Why here? Why was she here and not in the White
Street loft, but when she thought of the White Street
loft, really thought of it, Ned was in the loft, and he was
shoving her against the sharp cube that passed for a sofa.

She did not want to hear Ned, but she heard him,
saying, "My problem is I'm so quickly bored."

For a time, fucking, being fucked, being hurt, then
not being fucked. The astonished splatter in unlikely
places, red on a far white wall—oh, Isabel could be
bloody and dramatic, but in the end, Ned had outdone

her with his exit. *I don't want any of the stuff I've left. The car's yours.* Then he called a taxi to the airport. Now what?

As soon as she sold the car, she would go back to the White Street loft.

Last night she had dreamed Fife had drowned off a beach in Corfu but come back to life. Fife twisted in a dance and told her she was common, she was dull—cement had more color. How could someone as mean as Fife die? She had never believed it, his drowning, so his resurrection seemed right. Then the dream scene changed and Fife stood naked in a tub in a middle-brow bathroom, everything ordinary—a house some-how hers and he knew it. Oh, the self-consciousness she experienced in dreams! Fife stood looking out at her, making dismissive appraisals—professional name? "What profession? Unless you're doing business with your crease." She pulled the curtain across his face all the while seeing his face grow long and desperate, putty mobility with a hole for howling and then the tub broke apart and all turned black with the blunt conclusiveness she knew for hell. He fell before he had a chance to change expressions. Gone that fast, forever and ever. Amen. When she woke she was relieved, for how could she be afraid of someone who was dead to her?

★

At the Clam Box so many weeks ago Dinah had met
Isabel for the first time. She had met Ned, too, a girl
more than a boy with small, decisive features, sleepy
eyes, side part. Caramel as a color of hair on him looked
new; he was a sleek boy in an ad for cologne, ambiva-
lent or shy. Dinah remembered how she had looked at
Ned more emboldened than she was wont to be and
afraid. Over steamers Dinah told him she wouldn't
want to be any part of any kind of interview with
Clive, especially one that might turn into more, into
a long story, a novel, some sort of book. He had asked
would she talk to him on other subjects then, and she
had said, yes—boldly. He never visited but once, and
that, for the last time.

Dinah and Clive beyond the checkout at the Trade
Winds grocery resumed their conversation about the
Bournes. "How did you know Ned was talented?"
Dinah asked.

"He told me. He told me his agent was Carol
Bane."

"Who's Carol Bane?"

"I don't know. He said her name in a way that
made me think I should know."

Clive, in loose clothing, scootered the grocery cart and hiked on, a kind of skateboard, stuttering down the incline to the car. Here in the parking lot, in the yellowing middle of things, some reds out there, thrashed colors, his shirt was flying open; his pants were full of air. He offered his high spirits for the ride home. The anodyne of cheer; he said he was healed and whole; he lacked for nothing. And she? Dinah? Isabel, Sally? Who needed pills?

Sally needed pills. Dinah had seen her shake some out, not count, and take them.

"They seem to be working," he said. "She holds still longer."

"You are so critical."

He was not! He was lost in good feeling! He had his fox—he didn't deserve her. What a sight in the high grass. Years earlier a suggestion of horses in motion stamping toward the viewer, a palette of blues, whites, yellows, greens. Not much green, not like now; then his misery had been in the making of the paintings: to be bound indoors, tender treatment, on his butt all day because of a heel spur that had brought him to the ground when first he stepped on it—pain! A bone was broken.

"'Pain has an element of . . .'? What? No, I didn't forget." Dinah knew Miss Dickinson's terms for absence, emptiness, nothing; she knew the poet was well versed on the subject of pain and that the poet was right; the sudden erasure of the world so completely was a white astonishment. The horses were a response to that moment when pain felled him and the world was white. Sally had said of the horses, "There's a lot of air in the paintings."

He healed.

In this way Dinah and Clive drove back home talking about the fox, the horses, pain. Talking about Sally. Talking about Sally at the farmer's market with Isabel Bourne.

"Should I say Stark?" Dinah asked. "Isabel Stark?"

He shrugged, taken up by the effortlessness of his summer life in Maine. He had his health; his body worked.

"Sally says that despite appearances Isabel likes food"—good news, good news for the starving young woman disappearing before their very eyes.

A few weeks ago, Clive had painted Isabel, and when he thought of her frame in the window frame, the light so blue, he saw the window was the angular element while she was some pale blue strokes. The sky was alive; it thrummed against the eyes—God's fist.

How could Isabel have gone off the road where she did?

Shape, color, light, the fine details of a face were of no interest to him except to know now that the shape in the window had come to the Bridge House hopeful of repair and had been broken.

Longfield's Beauty
Maine, 2004

"Age," Dinah said. "I don't know how else to talk about it. I am not modern." A remark purely true just to see her as she was, Dinah, dated as a finned car in pants she called pedal pushers. Dinah said, "I still go to bed in mascara on the chance I'll be seen by a lover."

The possibility that Dinah might be as unfaithful as Clive had not occurred to either woman, or so Dinah inferred from the dead air. "Does that surprise you?" she asked. "A lover?"

Isabel didn't answer. After a while, Sally said, "Does me."

"Oh, Sally," Dinah said.

"Does Dad know this?" Sally asked. "I'm sorry," she said.

"We were talking about age," Dinah said, explaining the mascara business had to do with her horrible discovery that she had caught up to Clive in years. He had grayed, sure, but not collapsed. "Can you believe I was once Clive's student?"

The same downturned eyes whenever Clive smiled, but he didn't smile enough while she was a smiling idiot, a stained bone with unnaturally blonde hair. "Have you ever seen this color?" she asked.

"Your hair is white though, isn't it?" Sally asked.

"Careful," she said, taking a big, round ring, like a thistle, spiked, off her finger so that Isabel might inspect it.

Dinah had Isabel's attention. "Imagine me forty years younger," she said, and she made a doused sound of something hot hissed out.

★

Was it too early to drink? There was only the sun to go by, and the sun said, Fine! Go ahead! You must be thirsty! The summer porch was Dinah's favorite place at any time of day in the high season. Just the high season?

"The high season depends on location, don't you think?"

The first and only other time Isabel had eaten with Dinah had been at the Clam Box at a corner table, a room the color of wet stones, rigging, nets, markers, traps, and on the table a pot of steamers and a smaller bowl of sudsy broth and a bowl of melted butter. Steamers at the Clam Box. The stomachs, dipped in butter, insinuated themselves on the way to her mouth, ugly and lustful at the same time. Steamers for starters with Ned and Isabel Bourne.

"We were a little drunk then," Isabel said, recalling her confession in the bathroom: *I'm not the person I wanted to be.* That was easy enough to say when tinkling between stalls, wasn't it? Isabel had said it, I'm not the person I wanted to be, and Dinah had responded, Who is ever? Dinah had wanted to tell the girl then, I know and you should know . . . she wanted to say, If you're looking for someone to listen to you . . . Clive liked to think he was a listener. . . . Dinah had wanted to say, You will be hurt—but the poor girl was already.

Now she said to Isabel that her memory of the Clam Box was of a girlish woman in a rucked peasant blouse and Chinese slippers, especially the slippers.

"I've always been partial to them."

"What about espadrilles?" Sally asked. "What about me?"

"What about you?" Dinah asked and was out of the room before a rejoinder. She was going to make drinks, throw together an appetizer plate, a bowl of olives —whatever people nibbled on at this hour—maybe cookies? Maybe everything the girls had bought at the farmer's market? By the time she came back to the conversation, Sally had moved next to Isabel so to see the bay and the blue sirens on the other side, Acadia and island sisters. From the quiet on the porch, close, sororal, Dinah inferred confessions had been made. Isabel, perhaps, had cried; her cheeks looked chapped. Onto this stage Dinah carried a tray with a pitcher of New England iced tea and tall glasses filled with ice and stems of mint. Sally fished out the mint, smelled it, bit a leaf, said it tasted dusty.

"We were talking about relationships," Isabel said.

"Sounds deadly."

"How much can you ask for?" Sally said. "That is the question."

"Ask for as much as you dare," Dinah said. "I've seen the future." More than once she had taken flowers to Wax Hill. Wax Hill, where the old folk bumped against whatever was held out to smell. "Their heads are no bigger than hydrangeas," Dinah said. "That's right. Look afraid."

★

Goat cheese amid the three graces. Clive wanted to paint them as they were on the porch—his wife, his daughter, his sometime little-mistress with a governess's self-abasement. Christ, Isabel, buck up, he was thinking. He walked over to the Adirondack chair and stuck a pillow behind her back, propped her up so she could speak.

"That chair is too big for you," Sally said, and they switched seats.

The sofa was a better fit for Isabel. Everyone agreed. He was thinking of the composition now that Isabel was visible and his wife Dinah was at her drink, and Sally, his daughter, was talking—about? He could look at them or the cheese. So very pretty! Green sprigs and purple pansies, a fanned deck of crackers, a wooden spreader. Sally and Isabel had bought cherry tomatoes and a bread called Brot, thin shingles speckled with caraway and sea salt, also smoked oysters and smoked bluefish, olives, something tan, enough food to make a dinner but this was just to start. "What can I do to help?" he asked Dinah—pro forma, he knew, but intention, not action, was what counted, wasn't it?

"Sit," Dinah said, and he made to when he pulled himself out of the chair.

"What's this?" He backed away to where Dinah was sitting.

"I'm sorry!" Sally took the yarn and needles off the chair and found the basket she had come with. "Hope nothing stuck you!"

"What are you making?" he asked.

"A modest scarf?"

"In brooding colors," Dinah said and she touched his arm, and he put his hand on her shoulder and kissed her on the forehead. "Dinah," he said because he liked to say her name.

Clive might have said something to Isabel, but he had interrupted Sally.

"Sally has a story," Dinah said to Clive. Then, "How do you know this, Sally?"

"I saw them kissing." Sally pulled herself forward in the chair. "Her poor husband looks a little like Henry the Eighth; he has a beard. At least I think he has a beard. If he doesn't have a beard, he has a pointy chin."

Clive liked his role in the gathering; nothing was expected of him beyond sitting, which he did largely, an open-armed posture, his drink held near the floor. Summer's ease, in a soft, clean shirt, rolled sleeves, he saw the dark ropes of his arms were a lustful seducement to any Polly to be shoved against the barn. Somewhere in the house is a hat Dinah gave him, a straw hat with a straw band and a papery flower stuck in the band. August and he is playing Pan; in Maine, in summer, he grows younger. Where was the hat from? Where was the hat? He signaled Sally to interrupt and ask Dinah if she remembered where that

hat was. "Do you remember that hat from Mexico?" he asked, and he described it, the hat she had bought him from—where in Mexico?

"Which hat?" She startled.

"The straw hat with the cornflower," he said. "You bought it for me."

She sat up and made herself a cracker, considering hats. "The one from Mexico," she said, "from Zihuatanejo," and her distant face told him she was upstairs in the closet looking for the straw hat from the market in Zihuatanejo. "I haven't seen it," Dinah said.

"So?" Sally was looking at him, bewildered.

"What?"

"What should I have done?" she asked.

"Sorry?" he asked. Sally, holding an overloaded cracker near her mouth, what was she talking about? "I don't know," he said, which seemed to be the answer, because she began to eat. She ate the cracker—it looked like a hoagie—and made another, added an olive. Ate it, ate it so fast, he picked off the pansy before it disappeared, but the perky cap of the goat cheese had collapsed; it looked hot and the Brot had curled. His drink was some kind of foam. He left to find his hat; he wanted to find and wear it. He wanted to wear it enough that he would open the attic on the chance it had turned into a souvenir. Upstairs in his closet he looked to the back of the top shelf. He had so many hats! He put on the Borsalino and felt raffish: *la sua era una vita fortunata.*

On the curb of a street in Trastevere, a melon-shaped woman in a housedress, short gray hair and stick legs, flats—the legs and the flats he remembered because she was rocking on the curb a little; she was walking a black dachshund, a smoothy, without shape, like her. Clive had seen that woman more than once in Rome and once he had followed her, so mesmerized was he by the backs of her elbows—the joint a dark line as made with a knife in the middle of capable dough.

"How handsome you look!" Dinah surprised him.

He said, "I had forgotten about this hat."

"Better than the straw hat."

Dinah said all the things he had come to expect her to say; she, his greatest champion, devoted, careful, kind. How could he assuage the pinch of remorse over Isabel except to admit that what he saw of himself in Isabel's face had been flattering, yet he had abused her. He was vain, which was a failing, except that it had kept him in motion.

In an expensive store that looked like a bomb shelter, he had purchased a sweater for Isabel; nothing in the store suited Dinah although he had looked.

Oh, no custos morum, he, but a serial adulterer—
he put the worst words to it—selfish, insensitive, yet he
was not ignorant of Dinah's forbearance but grateful.
"Thank you," he said to all of her compliments. "Thank
you," he said, and he held her, repeating, "I mean it,
thank you."

The advantages of an old wife, Clive thinks, are
too often overlooked in the market economy. A sensible
old man is wise to hold on to a sensible old wife. The
younger woman does not know that drama is wasted
on an old man with cold mad eyes. He is careless of
last names, often can't pronounce them; nevertheless,
the young woman thinks she is known—why? She
is, as they all are, a fungible creature with the same
small disasters—sometimes a story. Isabel, in New York,
months ago, dinner at King Arthur's Court, said, "I
know a lot of what I do isn't interesting but every day
has its scene or two." How he had liked her for that
and her flattering appreciation of his work, of course,
her appreciation of him and for such slight returns—
Christ. All young women should ask for more. If he
had a granddaughter that is what he would tell her. He
does have a granddaughter! He forgets about Wisia all
the time.

He followed Dinah into the kitchen.

"You're not going to wear your hat?" she asked.

Not now. Now he saw the clock was pointing at the grill and whatever was planned he offered to burn it.

The menu was salad and salad, thanks to Sally, who was trying not to eat meat.

"Really?" he said, pointedly skeptical.

"Steak tomorrow," Dinah said.

Her answer cheered him. Here was an old wife who did not change an old man's diet even if the change was healthful. On the porch Sally was still on her haunches and eating Brot and goat cheese while Isabel was saying, "Yaddo to rhyme with *shadow*. I've never been but I know how to say it." Isabel had met Ned at Columbia. "One night after some reading," she said, "we all went to a bar. There was talk about the Rapture, and I heard Ned say he wouldn't want to be a part of any group that excluded his pets from heaven." Isabel said, "I fell in love on the spot. He was seeing someone else then. Early in the summer, when the term was over, Ned called and asked if I would meet him in California. He needed to close his mother's estate and his plan was to drive her car across the country to New York. 'Was I up for a cross-country trip?' I told him my suitcase was already out."

By the time Isabel got to La Jolla, where Ned's mother had lived, the house was down to a crestfallen assortment of Pet's lesser antiques and what's known in the business as smalls, in Pet's case, stuff that looked inherited but wasn't—lineage in the shape of silver dresser sets and napkin rings, a horrible accumulation of tarnished utensils, pickle forks and berry spoons, sugar shakers, candlesticks, salt cellars with cobalt-blue glass liners—possessions! Ned was crazed with it all, and he called Bertita, Pet's longtime housekeeper—Bertita, *por favor!*—who rolled the house into a U-Haul and drove it away.

Isabel's work was a dashed insertion in her story. She thought of herself as . . . well, she didn't.

Clive said, "You should take yourself more seriously."

At the table, shaking open a napkin, he saw Dinah had put cold cuts and strips of cheese near his end of the table that he might make a Cobb salad if he were so inclined. He ran four miles every day. He needed the nourishment. He never got fat. There was a blue cheese dressing on the table as well as vinegar and oil, and the blue cheese was for him.

"The strips of Swiss are Dad's, I assume."

"Correct," he said, at the same time Dinah offered to cut more. "No one wants more," he said, and he told

Dinah to sit down even as she seemed to be checking off items—something missing. Dinah went off to the kitchen and Sally followed. "What's the matter?" he called after her, and then after Sally, "Where are you going?" but Sally didn't answer, and now he was alone with Isabel. This was Dinah's plan probably and she had let Sally in on it so that for a while at least, Isabel would have some time alone with him and he, with her, before she left for New York, but to say what?

"Tell me about the car," he said, "your accident."

"I didn't drive off the side of the road, if that's what you're thinking."

"Then how did it happen?"

"Do we have to talk about it?"

"No," he said. "We don't," and he forked salad and chewed slowly.

"I should thank you," she said.

"For what?"

"I was looking for a way to be happy."

"You're not saying you're happier now, are you?" he asked, and when she didn't answer, he repeated, "Are you?" Isabel, seated in the middle of the table, stared at the table and did not look at him when she spoke, which made him angry, unreasonably so, especially if she was happy. He could see himself, a puffed-up poisonous frog. He wasn't happy. Fuck that.

"Look," he said, "will you look at me?" And he leaned forward and took hold of her arm, less than gently, and she did look up, scornful mouth faintly pleased and familiar with violence, the hurting heat and the marks left behind. Her expression only made him angrier but he'd be damned. Better to back off, which he did; he took up his fork; he resumed his eating. Then almost in a way of passing, he said, "I'm sorry." He said, "I think you are a capable young woman and deserving of a happy life."

"Thanks," she said, "you've been a good example."

"I said I was sorry."

"I mean it," she said. "You've been straightforward with everyone."

"You have to stand up for yourself," he said and would have gone on, but she was crying and apologizing for crying, saying she was a mess. Always looking for someone else to shape her life.

"I'm going to go back to New York as soon as I sell the car," she said. She told him she was definitely going to sell the car. She wouldn't get very much; she knew that; they had told her—shocking devaluation, but the car was old to begin with. It was Pet's car, the one Isabel drove cross-country with Ned. She said, "I don't dare drive now. I don't trust myself."

Now he was interested. "You drove off the road on purpose then?"

"I don't know," she said. "I don't remember feeling involved."

He should have stood to embrace her, this young woman some thirty years younger—they had stopped touching each other and grown used to it when he was still painting her. An abrupt if quiet parting: He was preoccupied, she was confused, there was Ned. They hadn't seen each other—a week or more, ten days? Once met at the post office, another time Trade Winds grocery—but not until the business with Ned had they spoken at length with any warmth, not until Ned's leaving was there reason to meet. Now Dinah, it seems, had adopted her, Isabel Bourne—no, Stark. Isabel Stark. She did not look like a woman nearing forty; she did not look like his daughter, not the way she was dressed: Isabel in loose braids and a T-shirt, a suggestion of tits—right word for what she had, next to nothing, snotty girls on this most girlish woman. He lightly tugged a braid. "You are very sweet," he said, "and I have been selfish. I want to make up—I should make up—with all the women in my life. So, friends?" he asked, "Are we friends?" and he put his hand over hers, lightly.

★

"Oh, Sally." Dinah smiled to see the happy pills were working and the shaggy girl she loved was back and making her laugh until her arm weakened, and the pitcher she carried so heavy, water wagged near the spout. "Oh, Sally," she said.

"What? I'm the mother. I can say anything."

But what had Clive and Isabel said? What did he say to these iridescent girls in their quick sideways flights? Dinah did not care so long as he cared for her chiefly, as she did him in their daily passing, bumbly as wasps, hiving it out, makers, albeit slower. Slower? No, like the good doctor-poet of Paterson, Clive knew he was "more attractive to girls than when he was seventeen." He took them up and put them down like a fork, as needed. The figurative paintings in June, then the fox and now, what now? "Will you show us?" Dinah asked. At the sweet end of the meal, Dinah asked again, "Will you?"

His work had not always been applauded; he had suffered and doubted. "My style lacks a champion!" Adoring young women helped as did someone else to do housework and mail, drive, and keep a calendar. Dinah had come into his life just as it was turning. Oh, there had always been yes, the yeses from a few significant others, although the lash of uninterest was the greater sensation; exclusion, the continuous drizzling misery of it, had been the weather in Clive's thirties and forties, but then, nearing fifty, it had happened. "Trees in Bud," "Morning from the Porch." Could the titles have been more significant? "Rainy Afternoon."

Now, no rain, but an awning of light under which Clive stood in the barn, not entirely certain, unveiling the lily pond. The lily pond was far from completion— purple wounds on a largely white surface—and in his expressions Dinah saw he was not entirely certain of this work. He didn't look at it when he was showing others. "The lily pond is promising." That's what Dinah said. "I look forward to when it is finished," and so saying, she saw he was relieved. He showed off the summer's earlier triumphs. Paintings he was pleased with—he said so. She was glad to hear it.

"I look like a shrimp in that painting," Isabel said.

"A shrimp," Dinah said, "wedding hors d'oeuvre of choice." She said, "I like all the angles, the different points of view," and then no more, but she walked deeper into the soft interior of the barn expecting straw on the floor and chaff in the air, barn smells and the sudden swallow. Where was the kitten with the gummy eye, the one she had tried to catch in another such barn in another time, as a child? Isabel followed Dinah as if expectant of a story or some remarks on what they had just seen, a naked Isabel with no pubis to speak of, and all the action outside of the studio with Dinah and the garden. "I grew up in a house next to a farm," Dinah said. "I found all kinds of animal life there—some of it alarming—once I found a dead rat the size of a dog." By then, she remembered, the barn had already caved in and the wood had turned silvery in places, in places dark, a beautiful carcass in its long conclusion. Dinner was over; the viewing was over. "Someone should take you home," she said to Isabel, and Sally offered.

★

Dying barns and houses, that's what Isabel was thinking about when Sally put the farmers'-market fare, along with the box of tarts, in the backseat of the car. Watching her move, Isabel had decided that at age forty, Sally walked in a way that might seem aggressive to some—it had to Isabel—but which had more to do with Sally's height, and was meant as a smaller approach. Nevertheless, her posture seemed abject, and once they were on the road Isabel asked Sally, "Do you consider yourself a guest at your father's?"

"You have to ask?"

"He is . . ." Isabel made a wavy gesture.

"Moody? It's no use talking about him," she said as if they had been talking about Clive for a long time.

Isabel was not so keen on the subject that she pressed for more but went back to the conversation about abandoned houses, the Bridge House, the barns. On the Reach Road Isabel was attached to an empty house the bittersweet had overmastered; vines seemed to grow out of rather than into the open windows, and soon it would appear like topiary in a rough approximation of a house. "I have no business staying here in Maine," Isabel said. "I've got so much to do."

"Settle back," Sally said and she petted Isabel's shoulder.

Settle back, Izzie was her mother's expression, and so she did; she sat back in the dark car and wondered at the sequined glamour of the controls, the warm smell of a high-end rental rolling smoothly over a ruined road of frost heaves and no one else encountered on the road.

"You're a careful driver."

"No one's ever told me that," Sally said, "but I am glad you think so."

Easier to lie when not looking at a person; at least, this was Isabel's experience; it was also easier to speak intimately, to say, "I am more alone than I am used to." She asked Sally if she would stay, if she would spend the night. By then Sally had turned onto the drive but not without responding, saying, "Well."

Isabel said, "I've got extra nightgowns."

"Really?" Sally said, sounding skeptical about the nightgowns—their sufficiency?—while at the same time following Isabel into the house and the kitchen. There Isabel set down the polished onions, the carrots, the dusky kale. The leftover tarts slid in their box.

"Would you like one?"

"Later."

Later was a way of saying yes, and Isabel said she was glad, she was grateful. "You have no idea. Thank you, thank you, thank you," she said, and they took themselves out to the rough backyard to look at the moon. Sally made herself at home on the bulkhead, and Isabel sat at the back door under the light on a steep granite step. "Somebody must have had a purpose. Doesn't it look that way?"

"Do you mean the moon," Sally asked, "or the yard? The field grasses were encouraged, I think."

"I think so, too," Isabel said.

"I used to be a not-so-amateur gardener, you know."

"I didn't know."

"I've not worked in years," Sally said. "I have a law degree," she said. "Can you believe it? Surprises me, too. Law and landscaping, there's a practical combination. It's been an awards show of disappointments, but you must know that."

"Honestly," Isabel said, "your father didn't say." Isabel would not repeat his brusque summation of Sally: my daughter with my first wife, a heartache. He had failed to mention his daughter was attractive, forgetting Sally's face to speak of her mother's wrecked beauty. Sally in shadow, flat on her back on the bulkhead, was a still, consolatory shape far from the violent theater beside the door: frenzied insects bashing into the filthy light. Even the cobwebs were black. She lived here, didn't she, hadn't she, for more than a few weeks?

Nothing a broom couldn't fix and she was half inclined.

"Relax," Sally said. "Come sit next to me."

A familiar invitation—and welcome although Isabel wondered just how much Sally knew about her,
and as she neared, she said, "You know about your
father and me, don't you?" She sat at the bottom of
the bulkhead with her back to Sally. She said, "I sat for
him when I first got here."

"Yes," Sally said.

"And it doesn't bother you? I mean it was brief—
and rather one-sided, but still . . . you don't hate me?"

"You sound like my daughter," Sally said and she
rolled toward Isabel, lifted her rump and brushed off
tree slough. Sat, but made herself small—if such were
possible—knees pulled up, arms around her legs, hands
clasped, Isabel's posture. Sally said, "I once met someone
at an AA meeting in Long Beach, California. We spent
a week together and on our last night—I was visiting
my dad and Dinah—she told me she knew my dad.
She didn't have to say any more than that."

Isabel said, "I'm sorry."

"You know, you could have a rock garden."

"No," Isabel said, "I could never." Not after the
snake plant, an impulse purchase she had treated poorly
—even contemptuously. In the White Street loft, the
snake plant stood in indifferent foyer light. Over time,
the poor plant could not be soaked but the water ran
through it: Isabel could lift all three, four feet of it—pick

up a hempen spike and all of the plant came out of its pot in pot-shaped dirt, dry and compacted.

Isabel asked, "What are you thinking?"

"I don't know," Sally said. "If you don't know what to look for . . . you need to know what to look for in a thing that's dying to know when it's dead."

"It wouldn't be the first time," Isabel said.

"What else have you killed?"

The shih tzu came to mind—and Isabel flinched to remember him and what she had done. The baby that never was. And G, and—but Clive? Do you want to show your husband what you can do? More than one man had asked. Now Ned had shown her what he could do—no fooling: In the few weeks at the Bridge House he was onto something his agent liked.

"I had begun to think Carol Bane didn't exist," Isabel said. "Why is it so hard to picture the people closest to us as succeeding?"

Sally said, "I don't know."

Isabel refrained from explaining herself. One day perhaps there would be occasion to describe some jobs she once took—typing Ruth Draper's letters in Miss Wilsey's punitively small but respectable apartment on East Sixty-eighth—but not tonight. If there were other nights maybe—probably. She had been a substitute teacher at The Spence School. She still tutored.

She had some stories to tell. Also secrets. Some secrets had to do with Ned, and the possibility that he might reappear and want to play again meant she wouldn't tell: two together sitting smugly, the solidarity of two in the midst of company. Their fantasy life together, crossing on the *QE2*—that game—and the invented Lime House in Hampstead, NW3, all experience delivered in such detail that the fictions seemed fact, and the facts? The facts insisted on themselves. They flew economy to London and lived in Golder's Green in an unnamed, floridly wallpapered, ground-floor flat.

Some happiness to start there, some of it photographed, then perversely put away. In the nameless ground-floor flat in Golder's Green, Ned and Isabel had pulled their chairs close to the plug-in coals and read and read.

"I'm not one for travel actually, but with Ned, I could go anywhere. I would. I did."

★

"Oh, God!" Isabel with a lemon under a knife, tea and tarts at midnight, had cut deeply into her finger.

"Run it under cold water."

"Oh, God!" She saw the blood run off, and she contracted her vaginal muscles as if it might help contain the wound. "Oh . . ." The sting of it! The cut! She didn't like the cold water and she swaddled the finger with paper towels. Meanwhile, Sally was after the first-aid kit under the bathroom sink. She came back with the gauze in hand and took up Isabel's finger and wrapped it rapidly, efficiently, like a nurse. "I feel dizzy," Isabel said, and Sally put an arm around her, and led her from the sink to the kitchen chair, sat her down, and finished bandaging.

"I'm taking you to the emergency room at the hospital. It's not that late and there should be someone on duty. Where are your shoes?"

The gauze had begun to pink already.

"Keep your hand raised," Sally said. "It's a deep cut. You may need stitches. This is the kind of thing I would do," she said.

Isabel found her slippers—only slightly surprised at being barefoot—let herself be led to the car, door opened, legs swung in. "Okay?" Sally said, and Isabel nodded yes, though the gauze had begun to leak, so Sally gave her the kitchen towel she had brought along in case and told Isabel to wrap it around her finger and then her hand. In this way she muffled the bite and tried to subdue the sharp memory of cutting herself. She thought of graver agonies—wounds, burns— incalculable affliction of the sort she read about every day, but the hurt did not abate. The finger was hot and it beat, heartlike hot and sore.

For the rest—the long drive, the parking lot, the waiting room, the frosty windows in ambulatory— Isabel let herself be led. She shut her eyes when the doctor took up the needle to numb the area and then a kind of nothing until she looked down and saw a turbaned finger puppet that grew sharper as it woke but safe. Sally knew her way around hospitals and did the paperwork—check-in, checkout—all the while smiling at Isabel, saying how much she liked being around someone more hapless than herself.

★

In the watercolor of the lily pads Dinah likes best, the lily pads are a congestion of greens with here and there a pink or yellow crown for flower. The sky is made of orange strokes; the white paper shows through. What time is it in the painting? Could be dawn or sunset. The pond is a party, present tense and happy, but he might very well have started painting it on one of his silent, unhappy mornings. The same was true for the nude paintings. What were his sensations when paint- ing Dinah in the garden as seen from the studio with nakedness inside this summer in the shape of Isabel? Two summers ago, it was Caitlin with the red hair. Caitlin's pubis is the same red, not quite a red, but an orange brown, burnt-brown triangle, very small, the hips broad invitations. Never on any of the nudes are their nipples largely, colorfully noted. A bright triangle, roughly brushed in, is the focal point of the nude model's body. As far as Dinah's concerned, that is. No, in truth, the dynamic element is really the color and the contrasts; the body, except for suggested sexual parts, is pink; the facial features are incidental; the young women—young women to her, to Dinah—the young women are shapes.

Some of what has happened, some of what has been written about her husband and his interviews have made Dinah cynical. His work has been described as "showing us voluptuous ease," but also conveying "a respect for labor . . . no doubt a residue of his own early years of physical toil."

Toil? What toil to be the son of wealthy parents who have made it possible to be an artist, a figure destined to be reliant on a trust fund so that a trust fund has been provided?

How old were the kids conducting these interviews anyway?

Dinah was thirty when she first met Clive in an elective course on figurative painting. He seemed very young to be a visiting professor, but he told her that she seemed very old to be an undergraduate. "Just wise" was what she said. She had left college after her freshman year to marry her high school sweetheart and fuck and fuck and fuck with impunity before he deployed for Vietnam. The year was 1969. The baby, if indeed there ever was one, died; Dinah saw blood, and after that more blood, unbidden, clotted, black. The high school sweetheart came back, and they stayed married for two years. Why? She has knocked against this question before and had no answer except to remember why she married in the first place. His body! His body was the first place. Lolling in the school gym to see him and then to lean into his body. Talk was beside the point. The point was his long body, the combative hardness of his muscled body, and the smell of his body after running when his T-shirt was no more than a tissue she pressed her nose to. His inimitable smell! She has not tasted his like and never expected to even as she rubbed against him when they were no more than sweethearts; she knew this olfactory arousal would be forever particular to him, James, Jimmy, Jimbo Card. And she was right.

For a time her name was Dinah Card and she was married to Jim Card, who called her Dee.

Now she is Dinah Harris and nothing of her hometown is known; she writes under this name even as she writes of her hometown. The baby who never was is an informing sadness, an ink that blooms on the white sheet.

At age nine she broke her arm playing a stupid game with her best friend of the time, Cynthia. Cynthia tipped a hammock hooked up in a metal frame by sitting on the end and made Dinah climb to the top of what she called the mountain. "Climb the mountain!" Why not go to the park and play on the jungle gym? "Climb it!" Dinah slipped, her arm got caught somehow, and she fell—she was never able to explain the accident; even the game Cynthia had invented was hard to describe, but she was committed to it. Cynthia didn't believe Dinah had broken her arm, but Cynthia's mother believed it. "Dinah's hardly a sissy" was how Cynthia's mother defended her. First sensations of mortality then, the start of the ugly years and trembling, Dinah, five feet barely-something inches, feared most people, men especially. Her art teacher took her aside for more than one reason; Clive took her aside, too, but by then, at thirty, she knew what

men could and could not do to women, and she was
not afraid of Clive.

Weirdly fearless—adventuresome?—Dinah was
the first in a high school class of fifty who dared to
color her hair, and in Dinah's case, blue streaks. She
drew on herself as she did on other surfaces. She was
on her way to mascara when she met Jim. Now her
hands sometimes shake in applying eyeliner, and her
eyes come out uneven and she thinks she looks tragic,
like a French chanteuse—black pointy lips on a sad
face informed by too much knowing.

Another version of Dee and Jim Card: a rusty
S.O.S pad disintegrating in her hand. The sink is dry,
and the refrigerator, emptied, stinks; elsewhere locked
windows, old air. Who left the apartment first? No
sequence but objects, scenes, his glove without its mate.

She doesn't remember Jim's voice though she sees
him yelling at her on the stoop to their apartment.
Henry Street, Madison, Wisconsin, around the corner
from State Street, the center of power: at one end of
State Street the university, at the other, the capitol.
Politics, their politics were diverging when she thought,
as lovers, she and Jim should be in accord.

Another time she came back to their apartment
to find a pyre of old books from courses she had
taken—an entire term on Shelley, books on Freud

and books by Freud and books with *dialectic* in their titles—all stacked as for a purifying rite in the middle of the bare room where she and Jimbo had once done everything but cook and sleep. He left a pack of matches nearby.

The books were at the end, at least that's how she remembers it.

But why think on the past on such a day—pink wind, timid sun—softness in all things? She is on her hands and knees on the granite terrace Clive laid out a long time ago. She is neatening up with self-abasing ceremony. Her face nearly touches the stones in sorting the weeds from the moss and fancy pussytoes.

Something else she was thinking—what was it?

At Scottie Rostow's party, she and Jim didn't talk to anyone but huddled, facing each other, knee to knee, arms around in a loose embrace, heads pressed together, a mourning posture, both of them glum. But a family's history of service in the Marines is not an inheritance to squander, she learned.

Something else, this: Jim is sitting on the plank seat chair in his mother's kitchen, senior year, track season. She practically lives at his house. She snaps the kitchen towel at his little sister and talks with his mother about him in front of him. He drinks a milkshake at ten thirty every morning. Nothing

sticks to him but it turns to muscle. He is sitting on
the plank seat chair and taking off his running shoes
that in memory turn silvery, melted and runny. After
his exertions, the muscles in his arms jump just doing
little things, like taking off his shoes. He is sitting on
the plank seat in a plank of light.

Clive walks carefully over the terrace, exam-
ines her work, says, "Good job." But the ache! Her
shoulders especially, she massages her shoulders until
her hands cry out, please! Poor, misshapen hands, the
fleshy chuff deflated, her thumbs have disappeared.
When she holds out a hand, stop-sign fashion, only
four fingers show.

"Look at that, will you," Dinah says, and he does.
He frowns and gives her his hand and helps her up off
the pavement. The deep imprint of her knees in the
foamy kneeler is a disconcerting sight—too mortal.

"It doesn't stop you," Clive says.

> "Plainness is the beauty of aging:
> cropping my hair, blotting excess,"

He breaks off from quoting her and says, "I love your
face."

"And my poems?" she asks.

" 'Transparent Window on a Complex View' "

—he exhales the title as if he's just eaten something airy. "Of course, I like the poems—I like them very much.

"... what was solid was miraculous:
planes of light, day-old eggs on a white dish ..."

His recall for her work mostly pleases and when they come to the barn bench, he is still plucking lines, and she is listening to herself and how he hears her, and it wins her over that he knows, better than anyone else knows, the great divide between who she is and what she has done.

★

"Wait," Isabel said, and she thumbed Sally's cheek. "Just a little ink. Pen, I think. Okay. You're okay. Did you sleep all right? You weren't cold?"

"Fine," she said. "How's your finger?"

Isabel held up her finger, a swami heavy headed and hung over.

"Poor little fellow," Sally said.

"Doesn't hurt so much, just sore. Say," Isabel said, "we've got those tarts left over from last night for breakfast."

They took coffee and the leftover tarts outside, and it was then Isabel noticed the birds. She was sorry to have missed them in the first place. Sparrows by the hundreds cheeped in the shrubs enough to shake them. She walked down the hill with Sally, delighted by the gregarious birds and all that was moving and inviting from the house to the road and across the road for an uninterrupted view of Acadia, a blue symbol on the tranquil horizon. She told Sally how she often took this walk and how she liked to walk, too, in the Seaside Cemetery. If she didn't get outside first thing in the morning, she would have trouble breathing. "True!" she said.

"I believe you," Sally said.

★

"Should I be laughing so soon after?"

The question was how did Isabel feel about the pink sands of Bermuda and Phoebe Chester-Harris on a half shell?

"I can tell you what Ned has to wear in the tropics. I can tell you he's unpacking some dead guy's seersucker jacket yellowing at the collar. But will Phoebe let him wear it? That's the question."

Did Phoebe have a say in her husband's clothes?
The last time Isabel had seen Ben Harris was at their
country house and then he was wearing Barbour or
something. Ben Harris was not a thrift-store shopper.
No dead man's shoes for him. Ben Harris in Bermuda in sorbet colors, easy anywhere and with skin
that didn't burn, whereas Ned . . . ah, he was such a
tender baby.

The Bridge House, on a scenic road treacherously
full of blind spots, was locally famous and Clive Harris,
she liked to imagine, was more than locally famous, so
that pillowy elements attached to Sally and, to a lesser
degree, Isabel, and the women lounged with ease in
an indefinitely extended summer. The queen of the
meadow was nearly gone. (Weren't the common names
for flowers lovely?) The roses had rallied and there were
days yet in 'Longfield's Beauty.'

Sally drove Isabel to the outdoor concert: African
and African American choral music in the field overlooking the reach. The wind was arctic out of Canada
and worsened. Isabel was wearing a ski cap; it was that
cold. An old man in an overturned poncho staggered,
blind and blown. The sight of him! And then the not-
so-old woman in a parka wheeling her own wheelchair
out of the field after shelter. The hood to her parka was

tied tightly against the wind and crumpled her face, and she looked angry, though the music was full of odd notes resolving. There were upright bodies of every size everywhere, dancing. Isabel watched a toddler on legs stiff as stilts scare his mother while older children skidded around picnics or collided on purpose, fell. A boy with blond dreadlocks played on invisible bongos. He played with such passion, the music might be his, yet Isabel and Sally walked past him and nearer the larger sound of the chorus. They walked around the huddled and dancing. Someone called out, "Holly!" and Sally said, "Someone's kid, I bet."

"Everyone's here," Isabel said, though she knew no one, a few faces, but there, behind the fat woman in fleece, was Mr. Weed. Even Mr. Weed was at the concert, and Sally, seeing the skinny man on a picnic blanket, said yes, sure enough. "Mr. Weed is such a nice guy."

Really?

"Holly!" they heard again. They saw Stephanie who worked at the post office and the lithe woman with long white hair who sold them the goat cheese at the co-op. Sally said her name was Helen Friendlander; Helen was behind the co-op's hippie baskets from Ghana.

But where were the black faces, the migrants who picked in the blueberry barrens?

Were they Haitian, Isabel wondered, or what?

Sally said, "The Haitians pick apples and the Mexicans pick blueberries." She said, "The Guatemalans and Hondurans are loggers. The lobsters," she said, "are for white folks to get."

Isabel blew into her hands to warm them although it was warmer near the prow of the chorus and Isabel was not so cold that she couldn't stand and watch, without shivering, as an older man danced with a younger woman. They were not married; at least Isabel thought they were not married. "But why do I think that?" she asked Sally.

Sally said, "They might be anything to each other."

They danced, this ordinary man and younger, ordinary woman. They hopped and clapped, hooked arms, and went in circles.

Epilogue

Aura Kyle puts her father's best shoes in her lap. He wore these shoes when he acted as a driver for Mrs. Pfizer, which he did with greater regularity in the last years of his life. A dark walnut color, the shoes are glossy with his care—they could be mistaken for new. Someone else would gladly wear them, but Aura knows she will not give her father's shoes to anyone. Heart hobbled at the end, her quiet father yielded of necessity and put aside his job and his uniform—the green shirt with the EBS stitching, the pin with his name, Dan Carter. Dan Carter, one of the many Carters in Hancock County, now wore clothes better suited for a salesman, though he was largely unemployed. At home and short of breath, he sat at the card table, sat for hours every afternoon making toothpick ashtrays and pencil holders. In a better world her father would have died at the card table in rolled sleeves and good shoes; instead, he died seated on a crate in the middle of the frozen lake. Ice fishing! Gone alone, he must have known

what he was risking, but why had his wife let him go?
Aura's mother called the boys for a search party before
she remembered he had told her his intentions, yet she
had let him go knowing, as she must have known, the
icy air would kill him.

The father Aura remembers sat at the kitchen table
polishing his shoes—these shoes, cold and heavy in her
lap. The shoe trees preserve their shape and cork the
ominously stained linings. It must have hurt to wear
these shoes, but anyone finding him in an accident on
the road would think he was a salesman, if not a banker,
when all along her father was a man who liked to fix
motors and get greasy. Ed Kyle is a dirt man and Aura
is wed to him and can say, not without astonishment,
that she has known him for fifty years, forty-four of
which they have been married.

Aura and Ed Kyle have a daughter, named Nancy,
who lives with a man from Brewer. They don't want to
marry. Rick's divorced, already has kids, doesn't want
any more. His children call Nancy Nancy. Why can't
they call Nancy something affectionate? That way, they
might call Aura something; that way, she would be more
to them than what she is now, which is what?

A puffball granny in a rickracked house or a crone
in a perfume of soup, laundry baskets stacked in the
back of the truck, full of sheets hardly slept in by folks

on zigzagging routes—Rockport, Belfast, Stonington, Acadia. The ghosts of them, those guests, who crackled up the gravel drive at night, expected, waylaid strangers. Once, a small woman, not so young, drove in, high beams wheeling into the outraged woods on her noisy approach. She was traveling with a German shepherd who slept in the car. The car was the dog's crate, she explained, early the next morning after she had walked him down the drive, along the edge of the woods. Duke or Buck, he was a savage-looking muscle with an oily coat, a prodigious defecator and marker—piss-bleached holes in the modest lawn. His owner left the car windows down. Did the big dog rove? The small woman and her dog didn't stay long enough for Aura to find out much. The small woman, who could have used a breakfast, skipped it.

What was that all about do you suppose?

And the two fat men who sang for their breakfast? Ed said he didn't know where to look when they started singing a medley at the table: the sentimental journey song and the other one, with the "yangy sound," Ed calls it. "Sunshine, you are my sunshine, you make me happy . . ." All and all, she and Ed have had some very nice guests. The two fat men in matching sherbet colors, lime and mango, they said, were harmonizers, barbershop type.

Aura surprises herself sometimes with what she knows. Barbershop quartets, for instance, she has never seen one but on TV.

An actress stopped once for a week engagement at the opera house. Three nights she stayed. The actress had rich friends nearby, but a B & B was as close to a home of any kind as she would ever get, which was pretty much all she said. She didn't have time to take the boat to Rockport or hike or bike in Acadia. Lobster was all she knew of Maine. The actress was funny on TV but not in life. She was one of those who didn't like to talk at breakfast but gestured for coffee and black toast, no butter.

That visit had made Aura sad, and a couple, earlier in the summer, crying—or the girl crying—had astonished her. Easy to be awed by extravagant suffering or bitterness—look at her own over her father and his disappointed life—but joy or the quiet delight Aura once saw in the softened face of a woman who knew she was watched even as she ate, watched and admired, to witness such affection of one for another, to see the kinder moments as she has, and Ed has, too, this was all and enough. Ed often acts surprised, not so much by her observations as by the thing itself—heart or goodness or whatever a person wants to call it. Plants, he has said, are nicer. And that's true, but, oh, she lets herself be teased; he likes to nettle her, she knows, which is another way to love.

The breakfast that comes with a night at the Wax Hill B & B includes vegetables and fruits from the garden. Yesterday she served a couple from Minnesota grilled tomatoes topped with browned bread crumbs along with bacon and sunny-side eggs. She doesn't squeeze oranges; she doesn't go that far—no fresh juice, just Tropicana, but Aura's mother! Every morning the woman found the time to give her husband and children four ounces of fresh orange juice. Sausages and powder biscuits were also a part of their diet. No wonder, her father's heart. Aura's parents were long married, too, and met in the same way in high school. Her mother taught sixth grade—spelling tests and prepositions, long division, Greek myths.

The Greeks, her mother told her, valued hospitality. For eating rather than feeding his guests, the one-eyed giant Polyphemus lost his eye. Pious mortals who stick to the code fare better. Like the poor old couple—what were their names?—who offered all of what they had for the comfort of gods in disguise: the best chair, their last chicken, the cask of wine now sour but the gods make it sweeter. In the end, the old couple are granted any wish—and this is the tender part of the story Aura's mother loved and she does, too—the old couple say we have lived so long together, let neither of us ever have to live alone. Grant that we may die together. So it is that in dying they have only enough time to cry, "Farewell, dear companion," before they turn into trees, a linden and an oak, sprung from one trunk.

Acknowledgments

For their generous support I am indebted to the John Simon Guggenheim Memorial Foundation, the New York Foundation of the Arts, and Yaddo; for guidance and close reading thank you to Rebecca Godfrey, Elisabeth Schmitz, and Will Schutt. To Nick Schutt for joy, thank you, and to David Kersey, great enabler, love.